CALL TO JUSTICE

D C Adkisson

Call to Justice

D. C. Adkisson

This book is a work of fiction. Names, places, characters, and incidents are a work of the author's imagination or are used fictionally. Any resemblance or reference to any actual locales, events, or persons, living or dead, is entirely fictional.

Cover photo by D.C. Adkisson

DEDICATED to
Bert,
Gary,
Howard--
those were the days my friends!

ACKNOWLEDGMENTS

Special thanks goes to my wife in her labor of love in helping to edit this book. She took many hours of editing and making suggestions. Any mistakes found in the book would be due to my negligence in repairing the comments and editing she has done.

Glory and honor must go to my Savior Jesus Christ for allowing me the opportunity to write and share. My main purpose in writing is always to glorify Him.

Other Books by D.C. Adkisson

Elias Butler series:
The True and Unbiased Life of Elias Butler
Mal de Ojo
Redemption
Outlaws of Boulder Canyon
Troubles at Gregory Gulch

Miles Forrest:
Return From Tincup
Winter of the Wolves

The Shepherd
Twisted Tree
Walker

Devotional
Trails in the Wilderness

D. C. Adkisson

The way of the righteous is like
the first gleam of dawn,
which shines ever brighter
until the full light of day."
--Proverbs 4:18--
(New Living Translation)

CHAPTER 1

I took aim at the grand prince of the forest. The Indians call them "*wapiti*"; white men "elk." This one was a magnificent specimen with massive antlers grazing as if he hadn't a care in the world.

After several seconds I lowered my rifle. It just wasn't in me to kill this majestic creature. Perhaps if I were with a crew of men, but being alone the meat would go to waste and I wasn't one to waste wantonly.

That old bull had lived a life out here amongst the towering peaks, and it wasn't in me to bring it to an end even for a tasty elk steak. Time would take its toll, or an Ute arrow, and death would eventually come leaving his bones to be gnawed upon by the wolves and scavengers.

I stood watching him walk slowly back toward an aspen grove into which he eventually disappeared. Back at camp I'd chew on a piece of jerky, but at least I'd make fresh coffee.

Until a couple of weeks ago I had been a deputy sheriff of Arapaho County under Dave Cook. I resigned with the idea of visiting the western slope of Colorado which I now found myself doing, but not in the position that I thought. A gang of outlaws had robbed a stage killing the driver, messenger, and two passengers. I didn't know the passengers, a man and his wife, but Bill Lowman and Lary Jacobs were good friends of mine with whom I had worked over in Boulder County a few years back.

Cook entreated me to work with my old partner Elias Butler to bring the gang to justice. I consented. I was going nowhere in particular. The holdup took place between Idaho Spring and Georgetown which was out of Cook's jurisdiction as sheriff, but under the auspices of his Rocky Mountain Detective Association the marshals of both communities asked for his help.

The stage was carrying a large payroll for the Argo Mill and Lebanon Mine. There was no need for the murders. I know Jacobs would never have placed the customers in danger, so the outlaws could have taken the money and run. Cook did mention that Jacobs, after he and the others were fired upon, was able to shoot one of the gang. I needed to hurry to Idaho Springs if I wanted to talk to him while he was alive.

Half a day later I arrived in the Springs and found the way to the doctor's office. When I reined in, I saw Dr. Willard Kincaid and Elias outside his office.

Kincaid nodded a greeting after I dismounted then said, "He's not going to live much longer, so you two better stand by his side if he regains consciousness."

Elias grabbed my hand and gripped my shoulder, then we followed the doctor into the room where the vile specimen of society lay. The Doc explained that Jacobs was carrying double-ought shot and the shot shattered the man's breastbone and deflected into regions unknown in the man's body, while pieces of bone were flung throughout his lungs and upper organs.

"I don't know how he's still alive, but there he is," pointed the physician toward the man lying in a bed with blood-soaked bandages and sheets around him.

The man wakened when we came into the room and he tried to raise his hand, but all that moved were a couple of fingers. Elias let me do the questioning, but it was hard to hear through his wheezing. We did finally make out that his name was Willard Leach.

With concentration and patience we found out that there were six of them in the holdup. He was able to sputter two names: Colorado Bill and Cooke Brown before the blood started frothing from his mouth. "The gang split...Leadville...Springs," he moaned. "Meet at..." then he closed his eyes.

"The leader!" I yelled. "Don't die yet! Give me a name!"

It seemed as if he heard me, and attempted a smile but his mouth was now full of blood. Lifting his head he hissed through bloody teeth, "Ipson Mc..." then his head fell back and he was gone.

"Ipson somebody," Elias murmured, then with his hand he wiped down his face.

Doctor Kincaid came over to toss the sheet over the deceased man's face. Elias and I thanked him then went outside; Elias walking straight to his horse. I looked at him mount and thought that it seemed a lifetime ago that he had picked up that nag in Texas.

"Guess I'll head over toward Leadville," he informed me then continued. "Springs. Think he meant Glenwood?"

Nodding I replied, "That would be my guess." He tipped the brim of his hat then turned his horse from the hitching rail. "Be careful of snakes!" I hollered. He gave a grunt then nudged his horse into a little trot.

I decided to get a few supplies then visit the crime scene. The road was always busy, and it was unlikely that I'd come upon any tracks, but a person never knows until he looks. I might be fortunate to find some, and I was going that way anyway.

There was a jumble of tracks, but I found a set that I saw continuing on out past Georgetown. It was among several others that stopped at the Empire cutoff with these continuing on. After Empire the road was not so heavily travelled.

I had no idea if they were from the men I was seeking, but I was going to watch them; plus they were headed for Glenwood Springs.

Back in camp I leaned against my saddle and chewed on a piece of jerky thinking of the taste of elk steak that I could have been eating instead. Thoughts of Lowman and Jacobs came to mind, along with Elias.

It was pretty cool as I settled in for the evening, the jerky now gone. Darkness came quickly and I put another piece of wood on the fire causing the flames to flicker brightly. Reaching for the coffeepot to pour a second cup I heard the sound of horses. Placing the pot near the flame, I made sure the loop was off the hammer of my pistol.

Several minutes went by as I sipped the hot coffee when finally from the darkness of the trees a voice rang out, "Hullo, the camp!"

I took another swallow before answering. "Come in a' show yourself!" I yelled.

He moved from the trees slowly on foot into my camp. *Vigilance!* I heard a whispering deep in my soul.

As the man approached the fire, I ordered him, "Tell that other fellow out there in the shadows to come in as well."

There was movement and I saw two of the most down-and-out men I had ever seen. Their hair was long, tangled, and scraggly. Their clothes were stained with sweat, grease, blood, and who knows what else.

"How about a cup of coffee?" asked the man by the fire with a smile. He was the thinnest of the two men. On his face he had perhaps a two-week growth of blond whiskers, and his weak smile revealed that a couple of bottom teeth were missing.

"Help yourself," I responded which removed the smile and brought a scowl.

"Don't have a cup."

"Drink from the pot," I responded lifting my cup to my lips while watching the other man edge over toward Toit, my horse. I set my cup down, wiped the moisture off my moustache with the back of my left hand and calmly said. "Your friend better not take another step toward my horse or that coffee you're drinking will seep out through the holes in your stomach."

He saw my right hand on the butt of my gun. For several moments tension filled the air. I had a notion what he was going to do and I was ready. After taking another drink from the pot, I saw movement in his eyes.

As he flung the pot toward me I drew, hitting the pot and deflecting it to the side, then shot at the man near Toit hitting him in the lower leg. The skinny one took another step my direction. When he saw I had my gun pointed at him, he stopped and put up his hands.

CHAPTER 2

I motioned with my pistol, an 1873 Schofield . 45, toward the one near Toit to come sit by his companion.

"Cayn't!" he yelled. "You done shot me."

Cocking the pistol I aimed it at him. It's surprising the influence of a cocked gun in one's hand. He limped over to the fire, moaning and groaning as if he'd walked ten miles rather than ten steps, then sat down.

Motioning again with my gun I told the friend to fix him up. When he pulled a knife from his boot I cautioned him, "Careful with that toad-sticker."

He scowled at me then proceeded to slit the wounded man's trousers. "Ah, ain't nothin' but a measley scratch, not even a hole." He cut off the bottom of the trousers then folded it over and tied off the wound to stop the bleeding.

Hesitating momentarily he looked at his partner. I leaned slightly toward them, pointing my Schofield. "Dangerous thoughts like you're havin' will get you killed. Just gently toss that knife on the other side of the fire."

There was hate in his eyes until I saw them glance at the barrel of my pistol. He was a good boy and did what he was told, then sat back and stared into the fire.

"You fearsome desperadoes have names?" I asked.

The one I shot was older and looked quite unseemly. He had a round face and even through a couple weeks growth of whiskers a scar could be seen on the edge of his chin. It looked as if the whiskers could not grow there. His eyebrows were as one; his hair was as mangled and scraggly as his friend's but not as long. When he moved I noticed that part of his left ear was missing. He didn't answer, only spat in the fire and glared.

The skinny, anemic-looking one quickly volunteered, "Wiggins."

Ugly snarled, "You cayn't stay awake all night. As soon as you fall asleep we'll slit your throat and take that nag of a horse."

It upset me some, the way he referred to Toit. That horse had carried me many a mile through the War and up till now. He may be getting old but he certainly ain't a nag.

"That's what I figured," I responded then turned my gun upon Ugly. "Only one thing left to do."

Their eyes became as big as saucers from one of them fancy restaurants in Denver. Wiggins cried out, "You can't do that. You can just can't murder us in cold blood." Even Ugly was doing some squirming.

I didn't bother to remind them that they had planned to do that to me. Instead I said, "Who said anything about killin'? I'd just be wastin' good lead and would have to clean my gun." It would need cleaning as it was, but no need to plug these two low-lifes.

Getting to my feet I stooped over reaching for my saddlebags. I wasn't about to shoot them, nor was I going to use a good lasso on them, but I had some piggin' strings in my bags. Pulling out several I picked out one and flung it over to Ugly. "Tie your friend's hands. Tight!" I ordered moving my pistol for emphasis.

He complied but when instructed to put his hands behind his back he refused. I had to give him a little tap on the noggin. He swore and spit at me. I proceeded to give him another tap and hit him harder than I planned for he slumped to the ground. I told Wiggins to get up and after he struggled to do so I motioned toward an aspen tree. He sat with his back to it while I drug old Ugly over to it and propped him in sitting position. After tying his hands I tied two of the piggin' strings together and placed it around their necks and the tree. Just as I pulled it tight Ugly came to.

Jerking his head caused Wiggins to start gasping and hollering that he was being choked to death. That set Ugly off and he started in to cussin'. I surely didn't care for it and knew I wouldn't get much sleep if he kept that up. Reaching down I grabbed the boot on his good leg and with some effort pulled it off. His foot reeked; worse than a skunk.

"Don't you fellas wear socks?" I asked. Giving his boot a fling I went over and pulled off one of Wiggins. At least he wore socks, well a semblance of a sock. I pulled it off then told Ugly to open his mouth. He refused and I gave him a little tap on the head. He was gaining quite a collection of lumps and still wouldn't open so I tapped him a little harder and when he yelped I stuffed the sock in his mouth. His eyes started to water and I thought he might be turning a little green. That served his filthy mouth.

Going back to Wiggins I pulled his other boot and sock off. He was much more cooperative and said, "No need to put that thing in my mouth, I'll be quiet." I thought for a few seconds and since he hadn't fussed or fought I decided to just tuck it under his chin.

"Now you boys just settle down and get some rest," I suggested then chunked the boots off into the trees.

After putting some more wood on the fire I eased down on my bedroll. "Sure hope one of those hydrophobied skunks don't get a whiff of your feet and come thinkin' its a mate, or a coon mistaken the smell for rotten fish. Why, bad as they smell they might even draw an old bear down to check them out."

Wiggins' eyes widened again and he tucked his feet up and under him. Ugly, well, he just glared, but I did notice that his eyes were watering. They couldn't move with their necks tied like that or they'd choke.

"Pleasant dreams, boys," I muttered smiling at them. I reckoned that I had won friends for life.

When I awoke the next morning there was a chill in the air. The heads of my companions hung down and I wondered if they had choked each other during the night. I went over to nudge Ugly. Opening his eyes he jerked bringing a yelp from Wiggins.

Seeing they were all right I pulled the sock from Ugly's mouth and he started spewing again. Some people don't seem to learn so I pulled my pistol and added to his lumps telling him to be quiet and dangling Wiggins' sock in front of his face.

"I'm freezin'!" Wiggins complained.

He probably was a mite cold in his bare feet. "Hard bein' a tough guy," I said as I knelt by the ashes of last night's fire. Finding some coals under the ashes I added some kindling then began to fan it with my hat. Within several seconds I had a small flame to which I added more wood.

"You boys behave and watch your manners and I may leave some coffee fixin's for you."

After the blaze started I went to find the coffeepot I'd shot last night. There were two holes where my bullet penetrated about halfway up on the pot. I went to the brook nearby to clean it up. It was still somewhat usable.

Eating a quick breakfast of bacon and a couple cups of coffee I saddled up Toit and stowed my gear behind the saddle. Ugly continued to glare at me, but poor Wiggins was desperately pleading. I left the pot with some grounds inside and the rest of my bacon.

Taking Wiggins' knife I thew it at the tree where it stuck about six inches above their ears. I had noticed earlier that the leather around their necks had loosened. Giving them a nice smile I went to Toit.

After mounting I said, "You boys work together, an' inch yourselves up a little at a time you can cut that leather string. Be mighty careful that the knife doesn't fall out of the tree. Oh, and you best not wait too long, I know the varmints will smell that bacon."

Tipping my hat I then gave Toit a nudge with the heel of my boot. It was my plan to be in Glenwood Springs by suppertime.

CHAPTER 3

I was closer to Glenwood Springs than I had figured and arrived midafternoon. As Toit slowly walked down the main street it was easy to see that there was plenty of construction going on. It was my first time in the newly christened Glenwood Springs.

It was originally a mining community as were most mountain towns in Colorado and therefore a rough and tumble place full of wickedness and evil. The new city fathers wanted to be rid of the original name of Defiance and were building away from the earlier places keeping most of the vice in the old town.

Accosting a man on the street I asked where I could find the marshal's office and the livery. He kindly gave me directions, and I proceeded toward the marshal's. On the way I passed a couple of eateries. I saw Toit's ears perk up and had to laugh at myself; he must have heard my stomach grumbling about the lack of food.

The town was relatively small, but I had noticed in my travels in the state that many communities wanted to take on the air of Denver. Leadville for instance, and Central City, rivalled Denver with opera houses, hotels, saloons, and gambling halls. It seemed that Glenwood Springs might be on the same road.

I pulled up at the marshal's office tying Toit to the rail. Entering into the outer office, I saw that the marshal had a private office in the back, and another doorway that led to the cells.

There was a deputy sitting at the desk with his back to me and continued to ignore me when I approached. My gentle attitude made me want to tap him like I had to do the ugly fellow on the trail, but I was longsuffering. It's just not good practice to hit an officer of the law on the head with your pistol. It might put him in a foul mood.

Finally he turned around after I cleared my throat a couple of times. I politely asked if the marshal was in his office to which I received a curt, "He's busy."

The door was partially open that separated the front office from the marshal's, so I started to walk past the deputy and go in when I was stopped. "Get away, he's busy, I told you!" even more curt than before.

I took a step toward him. He had turned in his swivel chair toward me. I cocked the Greener that I always carried and his eyes darted to it. When they did I stepped forward putting the boot of my right foot against his chair and gave it a good shove. I had planned on just shoving him across the room, but I didn't push it right and flipped him over instead. Guess, in all it had the same purpose. The noise brought the marshal out of his office.

He took one look at me and frowned. Well, I figured that was not a nice way to greet a guest, so I scowled back at him. The deputy was fighting with the chair trying to get up.

The marshal snorted, "Don't care much for bounty hunters."

Right there I saw that he didn't study a person very closely. I wasn't a bounty hunter and let him know it. "Marshal, I could care less for any bounty. I'm here on official business."

As I uncocked the Greener, I gave him a big smile. "You could think of me as an Old Testament Redeemer," I paused to let that sink in, if it could. "But you are right--I am lookin' for a couple of fellas. Part of a gang that robbed a stage outside Georgetown, killed the passengers, the driver, and shotgun messenger."

All I got from him was a puzzled looked. "Redeemer?" he questioned. "What does that mean?"

By that time the deputy had won his fight with the chair and was brushing himself off. I turned my head and nodded at him.

"Don't you ever read your Bible?" I asked.

"Bah, don't have time for that stuff," he grunted.

I took the time to explain to him and the deputy the purpose of the Redeemer and how he was responsible to take care of the blood-debt of the family.

"I don't have a family, but there's some men that I'm lookin' for that killed a couple my friends and took off with a mine payroll. We figured there were six or seven of them. I know at least two were headed this way."

"Dave Cook sent me on the trail of some of these scoundrels, my pardner is trailing the others," I informed him. I did notice a slight change in his expression when I mentioned Cook.

The marshal and deputy were at least listening now. "I've heard of Cook," he affirmed. "Go on."

"I'm on the trail of a couple of lowlifes that go by the names of Colorado Bill and Cooke Brown. I don't have the name of any of the others that may be travelling with them," I stated.

At that point, the deputy spoke up excitedly, "Why marshal, ain't the one that goes by the name of Colorado Bill sittin' over in a cell? You're in luck, Mister... He's dyin'."

He stood and reached for the keys to the jail. After grabbing them he hesitated and looked at the marshal to make sure he was doing the right thing.

The marshal nodded with his head, "Let's go."

The deputy opened the heavy door to the jail an on each side of the room was two cells with another one at the end of the room. There was no light except that which would come through the window that was on the door. For a certainty is was not a very hospitable jail; then, of course, they aren't meant to be.

All the cells were empty except the first one where a scruffy-looking man, covered with blood was lying on a cot. "He and another hombre got in a fight at the saloon," the marshal began to explain. "He sliced the other man up real good, but the fellow got off a shot. Hit this here Colorado Bill right in the breadbasket."

When the deputy opened the cell I saw that Bill's eyes were open wide and filled with fear. "I'm not gonna do anything to you," I assured him. "Just want to ask a few questions."

His eyes continued to show fear then he raised his hand to point. I frowned, looking where he was pointing, then leaned toward him. "Are you Colorado Bill?"

He began to sputter and groaned, "Get that man out of the corner."

The three of us looked in the corner where he was pointing. There was no one. My gaze lingered as I thought, *or is there*?

I moved between the man and the corner so he could not see his invisible invader. "Were you part of the gang that raided a stagecoach out of Idaho Springs heading for Georgetown several days back?"

He groaned now hiding his eyes. "Speak up, at least make your last few minutes on this earth count for something! Where is Brown?"

Lifting his head he tried to see past me, then began to mumble. "It was Ipson and Brown that did most of the shooting. I remember shooting the man in the coach. I hit him, but didn't know if I kilt him."

Grasping at his stomach he was now moaning. I could tell he was in terrible pain and it was not only physical.

"Ipson who? Tell me his name!" I ordered.

Bill tried to lick his lips, but there wasn't enough moisture in his mouth to do so. "McCracken, Ipson McCracken. He and the half-wit said they were goin' to Leadville."

"The half-wit, he have a name?" I continued to prod.

"Brit Londle," he replied reaching out one of his hands toward me. "Be careful of him. He's crazy."

"Where's Brown?" I asked. I could see that he was fading fast.

His breathing was shallow, but he got out the words, "Said he was headin' for the diggin's down in the San Juans." He then began to gurgle. I never did like that sound.

"Thanks, Bill. You still have time to make peace with your Maker before cashin' in," I told him.

With eyes half shut he looked at me. "Too late, too late to repent."

I reached down touching him on the shoulder. "Never too late," I said then walked out of the cell.

The marshal and deputy followed me out. When the deputy locked the outer door, we heard a scream coming from Bill. "He's comin'! Stop him!"

The three of us looked at the door with the deputy peering through the barred window. He turned to face us. "He had his arms out as if tryin' to keep someone away from him."

"Wonder who he was a-seein'?" the marshal asked.

"Good question, Marshal. Be a good idea to go read your Bible."

I asked where the telegraph office was, then tipped my hat at the deputy and walked out. I didn't even get their names. Oh, well, people come and go from your life, most of whom we don't know their names.

Going to Toit, I picked up the reins and walked him to the telegraph office, then I got a good meal at one of the restaurants. There was no need of me staying here any longer. I'd pick up a few supplies after eating and hit the trail on down toward Montrose. The San Juans...there were a lot of diggin's in those mountains.

CHAPTER 4

Toit and I moved along kicking up quite a bit of dust. I was in a hurry and kept nudging him forward. When we went through Carbondale, I slowed down just enough that we wouldn't run over anybody crossing the street in front of us.

At Carbondale the Roaring Fork River comes up from the southeast to meet the Crystal River from the south. I took the road following the Crystal finding a place to camp five miles or so from Carbondale.

That night I gave Toit a good rubdown for I had worked him hard the second half of the day. Darkness has set in before I gave him a bait of oats to devour, then I went about my nightly chores.

Since I had a large meal before leaving Glenwood Springs, I planned to just eat a light supper of a couple of leftover biscuits I had deposited in my pocket. I had picked up a new coffeepot and there was a need to break it in.

It seemed to work as well as my last one and soon I was sipping on a hot cup of black coffee listening to the river rush by and hearing the crackling of the wood in the fire. The sky was clear, the stars were bright.

After finishing the first cup and eating the two biscuits, I poured another cup then reached in my saddlebags for a couple of letters that I had. One was from two years ago. I had it memorized, but I went ahead and scooted closer to the fire to read.

I must tell you that Mr. Tomlison broke off our engagement... I realize now that I was a silly, immature woman. Spurning you for Mark was a mistake.

I didn't bother reading the rest. I opened the second one; I had received just before I left Denver. I smiled as I read it.

Miles, I must reach out to you. I am in desperate need of your friendship. I know I was a fool, will you please reconsider and join me in San Antonio?

They were both from Juanita. We, along with her mother, had survived a severe winter fighting men, weather, and wolves. I had hoped that there might be something between us, something with which we could build a future. It was not to be. I had written her a letter back in Denver telling her that I would always be her friend and maybe someday to drift down Texas way.

Finishing my coffee, I shook my head all the time smiling to myself, then reached over placing the letters carefully in the fire. As I watched the flames begin to devour them the paper curling into ash, I put an end to wishful thinking and to that part of my life.

I woke the next morning to a dreary, cloudy day. One thing for certain, riding the open country as often as I had, I knew there would be days of riding in bad weather; it looked as if this would be one of those days. I hurried to make coffee and fry up some bacon so I could get on the road and put some miles behind me before the storm hit.

Toit moved along at a low gallop sensing the change in the weather as well. Three hours later the storm hit. It was not one of those high country showers, but a deluge. I had been able to get my slicker out, but now it was coming harder and the lightning was flashing and thunder crashing. Anyone who has travelled the high country knows that it is not a good time for man or horse to be out. My eyes scanned the hills for a cave or outcropping; anything that would get Toit and me out of the downpour.

Finally, I found a place; just a little cleft in the rocks that went in a few feet. Enough to keep the rain off both of us as long as the wind didn't take a notion to blow from a different direction; we would be all right.

I dismounted going to look out from the cleft. Just as I did, lightning popped making me jump. I heard Toit snort, probably thinking that I was dumb to be that close to the storm. It was going to be one of those miserable days and nights on the trail and it didn't look like it was going to let up anytime soon. Life had taught me a lesson a long time ago—sometimes a person just has to hunker down until the storm passes, and that's not just a storm of nature. I really don't care for the smell of wet horse, but Toit was snorting every once in a while, so reckon he didn't care much for the smell of me either.

Sitting there is the grayness watching the rain fall in torrents, my mind began to wander. I had the opportunity to go to Salt Lake City with Lot Smith to hunt wild horses, but didn't care much for Mormon country and turned him down. I had thought about going back to work for the Rocking H, but once I left a place I didn't hanker to go back.

Funny how things happen in life, how the good Lord brings people along your path. Here I was, along with Elias trying to bring to justice those that sent friends and strangers to their death. I don't think of myself as the vindictive sort as I've seen too much of that in my travels, but there is still such a thing as justice. Maybe some would try to persuade that mercy should be shown, but I figured that was up to the courts. As long as I don't have to show them the Schofield or cock my Greener, mercy might be shown.

Elias, now Elias was something different. He was quick to action, sometimes maybe a little too sudden. As I hunkered down because of the storm I wondered where he was. I figured Leadville or maybe on down to Aspen. I sent a telegram to the marshal in Leadville letting Elias know what happened with Colorado Bill and giving him Ipson's last name.

Pulling on my moustache I remember when I first met him back in Texas. He's a mite younger than me, but a real go-getter. Fights that came to his friends he took mighty personal.

The rain was beginning to taper off some, but I waited until the lightning quite flashing. I was in no mood to be fried by a bolt. I had seen that happen to steers along the trail. Not a pretty sight, and the smell is awful.

Cooke Brown, and most likely another person was who I was after. Too bad I couldn't get out of Colorado Bill the name of the other man. Time would tell me who he was. I was a patient man, well at least I thought so, and methodical. I'd eventually find them.

After a few hours the rain turned into a drizzle. The lightning was no longer flashing so I decided to mount up again and at least ride another few hours down the road. Darkness would come early tonight, but might as well get a few miles in, and it couldn't get any wetter.

The rain and dark, brooding clouds made things seem dismal. As I travelled the muddy road, over to my right I could see the river raging with its new-found waters. It looked menacing, almost evil with the water rushing, now muddy.

I had been told that there were a few cabins along the way and that there was a small community at the crossroads, but I didn't know how far down the road they were. Night had flung its cloak of darkness down along the canyon I was travelling and the rain continued.

While passing around a bend in the road I thought I glimpsed a light. Continuing to move I was pleasantly surprised that it was indeed a light and, not only that, a cabin, barn, and store of some sort. I'd gladly take a night in the barn; soft hay would be a welcome bed, and at least I'd be dry.

There was no light in the store so I went and knocked on the door of the cabin then heard the scuffle of feet moving across the wooden floor.

"Comin', hold your horses!" came the voice. And old grizzled man opened the door. "Whadya want?"

"Would you mind if my horse and I spent the night in your barn? We're 'bout drowned."

"Well, whadya doin' out in the rain anyhow? Younguns don't have a lick of sense these days. Go ahead, there's already some other fools in there," he muttered then closed the door.

I had to chuckle as I walked Toit to the barn. I surely didn't think of myself as a "youngun." Upon reaching the barn I banged on the door as I sure didn't want to barge in completely unawares. Upon entering I saw that there was a fire going in a section used for a blacksmith's shop. There were three of them, and they looked the sight parading around in their longhandles with clothes draped around drying.

"Don't mean to bother you gents, but I'm in the same condition, soaked to the core," I told them.

"Nah," offered one dour-looking fellow. "That's Dutton, the other guy goes by Joe. That's it, nothin' 'fore, nothin' after, just Joe. My name's Brown."

CHAPTER 5

"Name's Brown," he said offering his hand.

I dropped Toit's reins then lifted the Greener cocking it as I brought it to bear on him. His eyes seemed to grow wider as he saw the twin barrels pointed at him. He automatically started to lift his hands as if he had done it before. Out of the corner of my eye I could see the other two, motionless as statues.

"First name?" I asked.

"John," he stuttered, "but not related to the other John Brown."

I lowered the shotgun, cautiously. I still looked at him somewhat skeptically. The others started moving, hovering around the fire trying to dry out. "Sorry, I'm lookin' for a fella by the name of Brown."

He let out a sigh and muttered, "Fellow, that sure wasn't a very friendly gesture seeing as we invited you to dry off and get warm 'round our fire. Why, land sakes, do you know how many Browns there are out here?"

I gave a slight nod, then moved Toit on through the barn into a stall and unsaddled him. After tossing him some hay I began to wipe and brush him down. He deserved a bit of good treatment carrying me all around the countryside. After I had taken care of him I went back to the fire and motioned toward the coffeepot.

"Go 'head," said Brown, now calm after his little scare. As I poured I had to shake my head. What a sight, three men in their skivvies and me half-drowned. I took off my hat; it sure had seen better days. One day, I thought, I'll buy me a new Stetson, but why now when I'm still wandering here and there?

Tentatively I took a sip of the hot coffee making sure I didn't burn my lips or tongue. It sure felt good going down into my stomach. I was chilled and the coffee helped me out.

While I was sipping my coffee, Joe spoke, "Why yuh after this Brown guy?"

"He and some of his cohorts killed a couple of friends of mine and two others while robbing a stage. Figured I owed them something, so bringing them to justice. Came across one in Glenwood Springs; he's now jawin' with the devil down in perdition. He told me where I could find Brown."

I finished my cup, then wiped my moustache lingering a moment pulling at the end of one side. Turning my attention to Brown, I said, "Fellow by the name of Colorado Bill."

"How many men were there?" asked Joe.

"Far as I can figure, six, maybe seven."

There was a grunt-type chuckle, "My land, six and you've only caught up with one. Not much retribution if yuh ask me."

"Fellow by the name of Leach was killed by the messenger, but he didn't die until he talked. But I want you to know I had no deal in the death of either. Colorado Bill had been shot by some drunk."

They all seemed as innocent as lambs. The three got out a deck of cards and proceeded to play for straws. I was invited, but told them I had some sleep to catch up on, and needed to be headin' out early the next morning.

Grabbing my bedroll I went over to a stack of hay. As I laid down, I heard the word deep in my soul, *Vigilance*. I kept the Greener with me, and did something I never had done before—cocked the hammers.

I don't know for sure how long I slept, but woke feeling the prongs of a hayfork against my chest. Opening my eyes, I looked into those of John Brown. A change had come over them; they once had been friendly and inviting but now they were evil and sinister. He pushed the prongs in a little deeper; I felt one puncture the skin.

"Name's John Cooke Brown. Just wanted you to know before you die," he sneered.

For the likes of me I don't understand why so many must tell of their intentions before they do it. Seems like they just have to brag on themselves a bit before doing an evil and cowardly deed. I felt it was my sacred duty before the Lord to ask him a pertinent question.

"Cooke, are you ready for the Judgment? Time for you is powerfully short and you might not get another chance."

This caught him by surprise. I felt a lessening of pressure as he drew the fork back to plunge it into my chest. That's when I pulled the trigger on the Greener. It knocked him back halfway across the barn. The sound of it jolted his two companions awake and I pointed the other barrel at them.

"Honest mister, we didn't know he was a murderer," whined Joe.

"He's right," stammered Dutton. "We were just goin' to stake a claim with him. He had the money for a stake."

There was something about them I didn't believe. "Dutton, you have a first name?" I inquired.

He looked at me puzzled. "Joe," he simply stated then explained. "Since there are two Joes, they call me Curly, or just Dutton." He then proceeded to wipe his hand over his bald head.

"So neither of you knew Brown before?"

"No, no, we met him in Glenwood. That's the honest truth," snapped Dutton quickly.

I had to grin as I thought, *What other truth is there besides honest*. Dutton answered too sharply; he wasn't telling the truth. Joe I was unsure of.

Taking the used shells from the Greener I reloaded when there came a hideous cry from outside the barn up on the mountain. "Lobo," stated Joe nervously.

I shook my head, "Death." I had heard that sound enough times over the years that I easily recognized it.

They were still dressed only in their longhandles and boots so I said, "You boys sit tight, I'm goin' to the store."

It wasn't five minutes before I heard horses running off down the road. I glimpsed out the small window of the store and saw the two "Joes" taking off, riding in their skivvies. It was a sight, but I reckoned they would run if they were guilty.

I purchased some coffee and grabbed a couple of cans of beans and peaches. Amazing what they're able to do now with these cans. Who knows what they will come up with next.

Brewster was the name of the owner of the trading post. I told him that Brown was dead in the barn along with the reason why. He told me that he would take care of the body and bury it.

Going back to the barn I saw that Brown's body had been rolled over. I checked his pockets, but didn't figure I'd find any money. There was a watch, a jackknife, and some tobacco. Checking his gear I found that his saddlebags were missing.

I had Toit saddled and ready within a few minutes. "Let's go," I said nudging him. "Shouldn't be too hard to follow those two." He went out at a trot down the road toward Montrose.

CHAPTER 6

A few days later I found myself riding into Montrose. There were only a few buildings thrown together, but it looked as if it could grow into a town. One never knew in Colorado how long a town would last, for in the blink of an eye they could turn into a ghost town. If a person was farmer-minded he could make a go of it in the land I had ridden through the past day; it appeared to be fertile and with diggings nearby could become a good supplier.

Looking around I saw an eatery, a general store, livery with blacksmith next to it, barber, the usual saloon, and an assortment of others. There was a hotel, but after looking at it I decided not to stay. It was just a large tent with a store front. I imagined they would soon be putting up a more stable structure.

I checked my vest pocket for my little pouch. I had five dollars. It would have to stretch until I found the outlaws I was chasing or a job to tide me over. I would forgo the eatery this time, but did go in the store to purchase some bacon and flour. There was already plenty coffee in my gear.

The storeowner and I chatted a little bit. He told me that there was a major strike down in the San Juans around Silverton. Claims were shooting up all over the place between Ouray and Durango.

When I asked about two men who might have recently rode through, perhaps in a hurry he said that he remembered them. They purchased some necessary items, but only stopped long enough to visit the saloon.

I thought he was going to laugh himself into a frenzy when I told them that I was chasing the two and that the last time I saw them they were high-tailing it in their longhandles.

"Better get yourself a coat," he advised. "It'll get cold up in those mountains."

I know he was warning me, but he was also looking for a sale. I had a good sheepskin coat; problem is that it was back in Denver. I didn't think to bring a heavy coat. There was a jacket in my roll and if worse came to worse I could wrap myself in by bedroll. This was still September, but I had lived in these mountains long enough to understand that an early winter storm could now come at any time.

"You'll make it to Ouray in a little over a day then you hit the high country. After that your travel will be slower, depending upon the traffic and the weather," he informed me as he followed me out of his establishment.

That night I camped near a little stream. I had never been in this country before, but the storeowner said that the road went to Ouray, a town named for the Ute chief. From there to Silverton then on down to a place called Durango.

Darkness came early back in the shadows of the evergreens in the midst of foothills. I set up camp. Fire started, fry bread ready to throw in the skillet after cooking some bacon, and water boiling for coffee. As I went to roll out my bedroll for the night I glanced up at the stars. I watched as there were only a few, then a few more seemed to pop out in the sky, then more. A couple of days ago I was in the pouring rain, now I was watching the handiwork of God in the clear night sky.

I made bacon then cooked the frybread in the grease then sopped the remaining grease with the frybread. There was a cup or two of coffee left in the pot. I'd leave it there and heat it up in the morning. That way I wouldn't be wasteful nor would I have to make any.

Toit was not far away. He was on a long picket so he could graze and also get to the stream. I felt a chill so I put some more wood on the fire. *I must be gettin' old,* I thought to myself, but I could feel the cold seep down into my bone marrow. That night I fell asleep in the midst of my prayer.

Waking the next morning I was a little stiff. Sometime during the night the clouds rolled in and there was a skiff of snow on the ground. Looking at my fire, I wondered if I could find an ember hiding down in the ashes. When I picked up a stick and began to stir, I was surprised to find some glowing remnants of last night's fire. I put some tinder around them and got down to blow on them until a flame burst forth.

If there was a skiff of snow here, what could I expect up in the high country? No time better than the present to check it out. I fried up some bacon and heated the leftover coffee. Not the best, but better than no coffee and then whispered, "Just a simple thank you, Lord, for keeping me." Within fifteen minutes I had cleaned up camp and was on the road.

As we moved up the road I saw that the sun was beginning to break through the layer of clouds. Soon it brightened into a beautiful morning. There was snow on the ground, the air was crisp, but my soul felt warm. In fact, I burst out in song until Toit showed his disgust by bucking a couple of times. I know he don't care much for my singing but there are times I just can't help but let it fly.

It didn't take long until we rode in and through Ouray. I didn't care about staying long. It wasn't any different than the mining communities I worked with over in the Front Range, only newer.

My, my, why didn't the good Lord allow me to travel in this area before. The San Juans are surely one of God's great cathedrals. Why that place, Notre Dame, or something like that, over in France can't compare with what God created. Such vistas, lofty peaks, canyons, rivers and streams. From time to time I saw deer and plenty of elk. This majestic scene took only a word from Him to create. My, my...

A few days later I was on the downward side of what was called Molas Pass. I had looked around Silverton hoping to run into one of the Joes, but something in me told me to go on down to Durango, get a job, then continue my search. I wasn't too concerned about food, for I could stop at any miner's diggings and he would treat me to some biscuits and coffee.

I was told by several that the best place to find a job was Durango, but to not hold my breath because of the time of year. Some of the miners were leaving their diggings already to look for jobs as winter came early to the San Juans.

It was definitely colder and there was quite a bit more snow. I could see where this would be hard country come late November; spring would be a long time coming.

There was quite a bit of traffic on the road with supply wagons moving up to Silverton and ore wagons moving down. Miners were moving in both directions. The two Joes must be here somewhere, but they had done a good job of eluding me.

Moving out of the canyon I came to a lush meadow with the Animas River flowing on one side. Durango had to be near. An hour later I rode down the street of Durango reining up at the livery to get Toit a stall.

The owner came out, spat a glob of tobacco juice and appraised me. "No need to get down. It's a dollar a day or five dollars a week."

I almost choked, "That's robbery!" I exclaimed.

He spit another glob, "That's the price; gold does that to a town," he said with an arrogant smile. "I have to pay more out for grain, so I have to charge more."

Touching my chest over the place where I kept my money pouch I knew all I had left was a dollar. "Thanks, but reckon I'll stay out of town."

"Don't hang around too long," he advised. "The marshal don't cotton to vagrants."

CHAPTER 7

As I turned Toit to head up the street I glanced backward and saw the stable owner hustle around the corner. Normally I would visit the marshal before any place else in town, but I decided to see if there was a newspaper. They should have news of work around town.

I was glancing through the two-page paper when the marshal showed up. "I have a complaint sworn out against you mister," he said.

Looking up from the paper my gaze went up to him. "What are you talking about?" I asked.

"A couple saw you riding into town then came to my office. They said you robbed them and left them for dead."

I laid the newspaper down and nodded at the clerk who allowed me to read it for no charge. "Am I able to see my accusers?"

"Come on down to the office and I'll round them up," he said. I followed him out the door, picked up Toit's reins and headed up the street behind the marshal.

The town was fairly busy with folks moving up and down the boardwalks on both sides of the street. We passed a couple of side streets then ahead I saw the jail.

Entering, the marshal held out his hands, "I'll take your guns now," he stated.

"Marshal, I don't want to be a bother to you, but that's exactly the only way you'll get them is to take them," I replied then pointed to a chair. "I'll sit right there until you bring those to accuse me to my face."

There was a chair with a stove across from it that had a coffeepot on top of it. I looked at it longingly. "Perchance you have some coffee."

"Go ahead," he said gruffly then went out to find my accusers.

Grabbing the handle of the pot I shook it to make sure there was some coffee. If was half full and I could feel the pot was still warm. On the shelf were some cups. I reached for one and filled it.

My mercy, that was the foulest coffee I ever did taste! I think the marshal must have washed out his socks then heated up the water. I headed to the door and threw the nasty brew in my cup out into the street.

I went back to the chair and sat myself down. It was a good ten minutes before the marshal came back. I was a mite surprised to see that measley-looking weasel Wiggins with him.

When they entered I stood to face them and almost laughed. "Where's the other man?"

"Couldn't find him, but this is the man who has sworn out the complaint."

"Well, you got me, I surely did leave them after they threatened to kill me in my sleep. As for robbin', that's a lie. They didn't have anything worth stealin'," I answered then looked to the marshal. "By the way, I don't reckon you have any jurisdiction over Glenwood Springs way."

He blustered a little, puffing his cheeks out seeking a good answer. "Mister, I don't want no trouble here!"

I smiled. "Marshal, I'm just lookin' for a job. Do you happen to know of one?"

"I don't want your kind here?" he smarted off.

Walking a step closer to him which must have frightened Wiggins some for he jumped back, I asked, "And what kind of man am I exactly?"

He didn't reply but moved away from me toward a desk along the wall. That left Wiggins in front of me. I turned my stare toward him.

"Marshal!" he said frightened. "Ain't yuh goin' to do nothin'?"

"Get out!" hollered the marshal. Wiggins jumped and skedaddled out the entrance.

Turning I nodded toward the marshal and started out. "Kohlmeyer might be hiring. Next road over and follow it to the end. He hauls freight to the mine camps."

I didn't turn. As I mounted Toit I looked around and saw Ugly standing down the road a mite. As I rode following the directions I was given, I pondered how those two miscreants arrived before I did.

There hadn't been any sign of Dutton or the other Joe. I hoped that if I could get a job that I would stumble across their path eventually. Breathing a little prayer, I found Kohlmeyer's place of business.

There were two corrals with several mules in each. Two large buildings stood there, one for his wagons and tools, the other must be a warehouse. There was a man standing outside when I rode up.

"Are you Mr. Kohlmeyer?" I inquired of the man who was standing there watching me approach. He was a tall, robust-looking man. Looking him from foot to head I saw that he wore worn brogans and tan corduroy pants held up by leather braces that went over a faded blue cotton shirt. His clean-shaven face appeared to have been chiseled from granite. On his head was a tan derby that had seen better days.

He didn't reply so I rode Toit a little closer thinking that perhaps he hadn't heard me. "Mr. Kohlmeyer, I heard you need a teamster."

Still without uttering a word he walked to me looking closely at Toit. He moved from my right side to the front, hesitating only a moment then to the other side. "Step down, we can talk." He then proceeded to walk to a loading platform and pushed himself up on it and sat.

It was then I noticed that to the side of what I took to be a warehouse two men were loading a wagon. They stopped working when they saw me approach Kohlmeyer.

"You always carry that scattergun?" Kohlmeyer asked with interest.

"Most of the time," I replied. "I've found that it can come in right handy."

He grunted then proceeded to look at me. "Ever drive a team?"

I assured him I had, telling him of my time in the Boulder area. He didn't say anything but I saw his eyebrows arch and eyes wander.

Turning to see what he was looking at, I saw Ugly approaching with his big knife in hand.

"I told you mister that I'd kill yuh," he snarled.

"Quit your jawin' and come do it then. I'm getting' tired of your threats."

I guess the way I was turned, he couldn't see the Greener in my hand. I let him get closer then swung the shotgun. It caught him on the side of the face breaking his jaw, and he went down like a sack of potatoes.

I turned back to Kohlmeyer, "Sorry about that Sir, but he and I have had some tangles in the past weeks. I don't even know his name, I just call him 'Ugly.' Sorry it had to happen in front of your place of business."

"Mister, I told you about causing trouble here." I turned to see the marshal along with Wiggins trailing behind him.

Wiggins started shouting," He hit him, Marshal. He had no cause to do it. He has been hassling us for weeks!"

I gave Wiggins a stare and he slunk behind the marshal.

"Give me the shotgun and your gunbelt; you're coming with me."

It was tense for a few moments as everyone saw my hesitation. Then Kohlmeyer blurted out, "Marshal, the man came at him with a knife. He had every right to protect himself. In fact, if'n it had been me I'd have killed the man."

"Give me the shotgun!" the marshal ordered again.

"Mister Kohlmeyer would you look after this piece for me? It was a gift from Dave Cook and I surely would hate to see it get lost somewhere."

As I handed the Greener toward Kohlmeyer he questioned, "Cook. You know Dave Cook?"

"Friend of mine," I answered. "I worked for him up in Boulder County for a spell. Then was a deputy for him in Arapaho County."

"He's coming with me," said the Marshal. "I'll send someone for your horse to put him in the stable."

I gave the marshal my gunbelt then looked at Mr. Kohlmeyer. "All right if I leave my horse with you as well. It's robbery the price they're charging at the stable."

He laughed then sprung from the platform taking the shotgun. "Sure 'nough. Tomorrow I'll come and throw your bail. You have a job and were protectin' yourself, and I'm an eyewitness. They can't hold you," Kohlmeyer declared looking right at the marshal.

"Thanks, I appreciate it." I stepped toward Wiggins and he jumped back. "Let's go, Marshal."

"Mister, you shouldn't be smiling like that. There are still charges against you."

I smiled then watched Kohlmeyer stoop down to look at the unconscious man. "You're right," he muttered. "He sure is ugly."

Wiggins stood there not knowing what to do. He wasn't strong enough to carry Ugly somewhere, and he saw that Kohlmeyer wasn't going to help as he had turned to join his two workers.

The marshal and I started out toward the jail and I thought to myself, *the Lord sure does work in mysterious ways.* Not only did I get a job, but now I get a free meal and a warm bed for the night. Yep, the six-bits in my pocket will keep for another day.

CHAPTER 8

I looked at the cells, not very pleasant. There were two cells with a small aisle between them. The cells were long and narrow and each had a rickety cot that were probably full of bedbugs. In one cell, an old fellow was laying on one of them.

The marshal put me in the cell with the man. "Looks like he has the only bed in the cell. Sorry, about that," laughed the marshal. "We start bringing in the drunk and disorderly about three hours from now. I'll fill the other cell up first." He turned then stopped to look at me. "Sleep well, oh, and by the way, enjoy your stay. City business isn't open on Sundays so you'll be here at least until Monday." He was cackling as he left.

Well I'm mighty glad I was able to give him some mirth over my situation. I looked at the far corner, away from the jail door checking it for bugs and spiders. It was dim in the room as there were only two barred windows high on the wall. Pretty soon I knew it would be dark. Sitting in the corner I did some pondering on the life of Joseph. It was the first time I had thought of the Good Book from a jail cell; it sure gives one a different perspective.

The old man in the cot rolled over, coughed, then looked at me. "Wha'd'they get you for?" He asked. "Gotta be careful in this here town. The marshal likes to show that he's cock of the walk."

"So is that what happened to you?"

"No siree, I happen to have a real crime to my charge. Caught my podner stealin' from our diggin's. Shot him outright. Nope, I'm in here on murder," he informed me proudly.

I pulled at the end of my moustache. "If you caught him stealin', why did they arrest you for murder?"

"Well, friend, he was on friendly terms with ol' T. Garten, that's the marshal. Plus no one could prove that my podner was stealin'," replied the convicted man.

He sat up to get a better look at me. "Yes, siree, next Thursday will be my last day here on this earth. By the way, things get a little cozy on a Saturday night when they start throwing in the drunks."

At least I had one hot meal today, but had to empty my pockets so now I didn't even have a penny to my name. The marshal took my pouch that contained six-bits and my jackknife. I'd left my saddlebags and gear with Kohlmeyer.

"Ol' Bull, that's what they call the marshal, has two deputies. Both still wet behind the ears. They think they're gunmen. Bah, I've seen some men that could outdraw them in their sleep," he paused and seemed to think. "By the way, we get breakfast between eight and nine."

It was dark when they started bringing the drunks in. The only light there was came from a dimly-lit lantern that was visible through the window of the jail door.

The first two were brought in by a deputy who deposited them on the floor of the cell across from me where they immediately began snoring. Throughout the rest of the night men were brought in and tossed in the same cell until there were ten men in it in various states of intoxication.

It must have been along toward midnight the marshal and another deputy returned with three more men in tow. He ordered my companion off the cot and threw one of the men down on it. Another man, that didn't appear too drunk went over to the cot to check on his partner.

"Marshal," the man hollered, "you didn't have to hit him that hard. He needs a doctor; he's bleeding pretty bad."

The marshal gave a little grunt and went out. I got up from my spot to have a look. There was blood all over the man's head and face. I touched his head and he gave out a gasp. It was hard to tell in the dark, but I believed that his skull was cracked. I started yelling for the marshal to come in, or someone. They wouldn't leave prisoners unattended, would they?

Finally a deputy came in and told me to pipe down.

"This man needs a doctor in a bad way," I informed him.

"He can wait until he sobers up tomorrow," came his curt reply.

"If he doesn't see a doctor, he might not have a tomorrow. His skull is split open." The deputy walked out; there was little I could do. I didn't even have a way to clean him up.

Looking at the man beside the one on the cot, I asked, "What's his name?"

"Lyle Mercer," came the reply. "Folks call me 'Slim,' he paused. I could tell he was looking down at his friend. "Thanks for tryin'."

I went back to my corner. Sitting there in the dark I began to think of the disciples. Those ol' boys were in and out of jail a number of times. I tried to remember the things they did. They prayed, for sure, they smiled at their predicament, and whenthey sang.

We were a couple of months from Christmas, but I started singing as loud as I could, "Silent night! Holy night! All is calm..." The man on death's row joined in with me. Soon there were several in the jail singing along. I figured most of them knew "Silent Night."

Now the earth didn't shake, nor the jail cell open, but that marshal and deputy came rushing in. "Shut your mouths!" the marshal exclaimed.

"Just singin' a little Christmas song to bring joy and cheer into these dreary cells. By the way, you need to take this man to the doctor or he'll be dead by mornin' and you'll have a dozen or more witnesses against you for cruel and unusual punishment."

He muttered a few words not fit to repeat then opened the cell. He had the deputy haul the man out even allowing his friend to help. The marshal had his gun out holding it on the convicted man and myself.

After the marshal left, the old man reclaimed his cot then called out to me asking if I would sing again. Now, I ain't ever had that happen before. I told him sure if he and the others would join me. I tell you we sang "Silent Night" a dozen or more times and other Christmas songs we could remember. I think ol' Paul and Silas knew a thing or two. I also knew that I wouldn't be getting out until Monday, but that meant at least three more meals.

CHAPTER 9

True to his word, Kohlmeyer came and produced my bail early Monday. The marshal gave me a stern warning not to leave town until my hearing. I looked him in the eye shaking my head. Walking out of the jail, I was greeted with a wind that cut through me causing me to shudder.

Kohlmeyer must have noticed. "Let's go over and have some breakfast. I'll pay."

Normally I'm not one to take handouts, but over the years I've learned that the good Lord sends people around to help us and we shouldn't rob those who are trying to help of a blessing. The muddy streets we had to cross were full of ruts. Wearing my boots didn't help me much, but at least kept the water and mud from oozing in. I pulled my jacket collar up but it did little to ward off the cold.

There was little movement on this chilly Monday morning. Kohlmeyer led me to a little corner cafe a block off mainstreet. "Molly's Kitchen" was the sign over the door.

Entering the room, the chill almost immediately left, but my feet were still cold. I nodded at a couple of miners that sat nursing their coffee, and followed Kohlmeyer over to a table near the stove.

"Molly, bring us some of that belly-wash," he hollered, "and fix us some hen's fruit, taters and a couple steaks!"

Now, I wasn't going to argue with a man if he wanted to buy a breakfast like that, but thought it only fair to reserve judgment on the coffee until I had my fair share. Kohlmeyer smiled as I sat close to the stove to warm up my feet. The place was simple and rustic with quaint, checkered tablecloths on each table, and I might add, clean ones. That made me feel good for that meant the coffee cups were probably clean as well.

"This place belongs to Molly and her mother. Molly's father is one of my teamsters and often in a pinch will run one of the stores I have in the mountains. Right now he's up at Silverton. I have a man who is recuperating from a broken leg that will work it as soon as he is able to be up and moving around. Molly's father don't allow the women up near the diggin's."

"Wise man," I muttered.

My feet were beginning to warm up when I looked up to see a dark-haired gal come from the kitchen carrying two cups and a pot of coffee. She set the cups down and filled each. "Miles, this here is the prettiest gal in the San Juans; and she bakes a mighty tasty pie as well. One bite and you'd think you tasted something right from the kitchens of Heaven."

With that she blushed, and slapped at Kohlmeyer with the towel she had with her. I saw her glance my way and our eyes locked for an instant, then she turned to walk back to the kitchen when Kohlmeyer grabbed her arm, "Leave the pot on the stove, dear."

We sat and drank coffee while he told me what he expected on the job. I was hired to be a teamster and sometimes guard. It was mighty good pay; two dollars a day, and if I rode guard then the mines would pay extra and sometimes Wells Fargo kicked in some. The man was on top of things. He told me he had telegraphed Dave Cook and had already heard back with a reference, and also had a message for me--Elias was in Denver.

It wasn't long before Molly brought the steaks, eggs, and potatoes along with a plate of biscuits. Been a while since I ate that much, but my innards were telling me to hurry up and give it a try.

"Mister Miles, how long to you plan on being here in Durango?" Molly asked, giving Kohlmeyer a dirty look since he hadn't properly introduced us.

"It's Forrest, ma'am, Miles Forrest, and you can call me Miles. Right now..." I paused twisting at the end of my moustache. "I really don't know. I should go back to Denver in the spring, but who knows, I may take a hankerin' to lookin' at the backsides of mules."

She giggled, then glared at Kohlmeyer again. He sort of cringed from that look. Turning to me, she smiled, "It's not ma'am, Mr. Forrest. If I'm to call you Miles, then I expect to hear Molly come from your lips."

Looking over her shoulders as she walked away, I saw a smile then quickly she flicked the towel at Kohlmeyer again before going over to clean up the table where the two miners had been sitting.

"Feisty sort, ain't she," I stated. "Mister Kohlmeyer, you've done a lot for me already, but could I ask yuh if I could leave my horse in your corral? And, well, one more thing, would it be all right if I bunk in the stable? Right now I'm a little stretched on cash."

I thought I should tell him why I was really in Durango. Right now would be a good time, but before I could start, he answered me. "Sure 'nough. In fact there is a little room off the barn with a bed and stove in it. Be a good place for you to throw your belongings. I'll take the rent out of your check; how's four dollars a month sound for both you and your horse? Plus, you ain't going in those mountains without a coat. Go on down to the emporium and pick out yourself a coat and put it on my tab." Then he reached out his hand.

"Mind if I see about a couple of things? It won't take long, but I wonder if you could tell me where I could find a judge?"

He jerked back with a start when I said I wanted to see a judge. I smiled. "There was a man in my cell that is supposed to hang come Thursday, and also on Saturday night a man was thrown in with a cracked skull."

Rubbing his fingers on his chin a few times, he answered, "Judge Klasco is probably in his office." After giving me directions he said, "Don't take too long. I want to load up the wagons so you can head out early in the morning. Need to get this freight up to Silverton before a big snow."

I found the Judge to be an amiable man. He informed me that the case on Mr. Gifford had not come up before him. I was told by the Judge that he would temporarily commute the sentence until he could look into it further and also check on the man with the cracked skull.

The weeks rolled by as I worked daily either driving one of the wagons or riding guard. I still hadn't seen anything of Dutton or Joe and was keeping Cook informed. Until otherwise directed, I was to stay in the Silverton/Durango area.

Christmas was almost upon us. I was mulling that thought over as our little convoy of four wagons was headed to Silverton. There had been quite a bit of snow in the high country, but workers were able to keep the passes open. If weather didn't catch us, we should be back on the twenty-seventh of the month.

There was only a skim of snow on the ground when we left Durango and not a cloud in the sky. It was up to around forty degrees so the road was muddy. Working the team gave me plenty of time to ponder over the idea of Christmas. I thought of the baby Jesus and also of some of my past Christmases. Being in the mountains and the snow with the cold temperatures, I also thought of the winter with Juanita.

We pulled in to stop for the second night. As we were getting the necessities ready for camp I could hear the men grumbling about missing Christmas. It was typical of working men. The funny thing is that most of them would spend Christmas alone as they didn't have wives or families.

I had the fire going, and Fresno was getting coffee ready when five riders came up to our camp. My hand went to the Greener that was laying on the ground next to me. Wiggins and Ugly were in the group.

"Mind if we share your fire for the night?" a rugged-looking rider asked.

"Keep ridin'," I ordered.

I was the newest hire and it wasn't really my position to be giving orders, but I wasn't challenged. The man who had spoke just nodded his head and they took off up the road. Wiggins and Ugly glared at me when they rode by. I went back to my chores; however, I noticed that the teamsters were all eyeing me, but said nothing.

We arrived, unloaded, and made it back to Durango the afternoon of the twenty-seventh. Kohlmeyer had men there ready to unhitch and take care of the mules. The men drifted off to the saloons or to their shanty. I had already decided to go celebrate Christmas by going over to Molly's eatery.

Sitting there in the comfortable room I enjoyed my coffee. I thought of the time when my feet were near frozen and smiled at the comfort of the stove knowing my toes were happy. Life was good. A meal of steak, onions, and potatoes was a change from the fare I had on several Christmases. However, over the years I had learned to be grateful for whatever was on the table.

Molly interrupted me by placing a large piece of mincemeat pie in front of me. "Merry Christmas," she said. "Sorry if it's a few days late."

"Oh my, what did I do to deserve this?" I asked looking at her—she blushed.

"Nothing...shouldn't ask a woman why she does something for a man," then she smiled going back to the kitchen.

I almost moaned as I sunk my teeth into it; or perhaps I did for she came from the kitchen with the other half of the pie for me to take back to my room with me. Had she already found out my weakness for pie?

"When do you head back to Silverton?" she asked. "I heard you were taking a wagon back to the camps and would ride as guard on a shipment coming back to Durango."

"Day after tomorrow, first light," I replied. "We'll load tomorrow; we need to make one more trip before the passes are closed," I said then shook my head. "I surely don't know how those miners make it during the winter."

"Gold gets into a man's system," she said quietly.

"Well, I've never had that problem. Never been bitten by the gold bug. I don't reckon it's gold that makes a man rich."

She smiled, "You're a rare one. Come by before you leave and I'll have some biscuits for you to take."

Sitting in my little room that night, I ate another piece of pie before going to bed. I was working my mind over something she said about me being *a rare one*. What did she mean? Ahh, I'm making too much of a little statement.

Before I laid down, I looked outside. It had begun to snow.

CHAPTER 10

I reached between my feet into the sack to grab one of the biscuits Molly made me. It was not only a tasty biscuit but she put bacon in it. As I chewed I thought of the hand that accidentally touched mine when she handed me the sack.

Funny how time changes things. A couple of years ago I was close to freezing to death, I had been attacked by wolves, and then faced the guns of two-legged critters. Now, I'm still looking for the two-legged variety of animals, but most of the time I'm fairly warm. I had put Juanita on a train heading for Texas with her new beau. I was supposed to meet her last June in Denver, but she never showed up, then I received a letter saying that she wanted me to come to Texas. Hmm, now I had been given a smile and a mincemeat pie.

The traveling was good despite there being snow on the ground. The road was still open though we did have to stop a time or two to dig through drifts. Benj Muncke, a man built like a brick was the head of the guards and he took the lead. There were five wagons with a guard on each and I brought up the rear riding on Toit. Though the road was open, it was still slow going through the snow with the heavily loaded wagons.

There really was no need for the extra guards going up to Silverton. They were there for the return trip. It took two days to unload then go to the different mines to load up the ore. The wagons were three times as heavy now; Muncke decided to bring extra mules in case they were needed to haul the extra load up the passes.

We were about halfway down Coal Bank Pass when they hit us. I had dropped back to check on Toit's leg as he was developing a slight limp. As I was examining his leg I heard a shot from around the bend in front of me. Mounting up, I moved slowly toward the sound not wanting to rush into a mess of bullets. One guard was down and the driver, along with the other guards had their hands up.

I didn't see any need to be wasting time. "Yeehaw!" I yelled and spurred Toit. Firing one barrel from the Greener my bullet struck one of the attackers square in the chest and knocked him out of his saddle. The second man went down with the load from the other barrel. This started quite a commotion; they were totally surprised. I reckoned they didn't know I was back around the bend.

The other guards and Muncke swung into action and began to fire. I turned Toit and saw him about the same time he saw me—Ugly.

He started riding toward me. I tossed the Greener aside then pulled my pistol. Ugly was firing and I felt the tug of a bullet as it struck my shoulder. As we rode closer to each other, I could hear him clicking on empty chambers. Toit was moving fast and I took aim. As I shot, Toit slipped on ice beneath the snow. Falling, I saw Ugly smile then a surprised look came upon his face as his horse went down.

It was over in a few seconds. We had one guard killed and another wounded. Toit was up, and other than a limp seemed all right.

I walked toward Muncke. From behind me I heard a mumbled voice, "I told you I'd kill you."

Turning I saw Ugly with his pistol pointing directly at me. Funny how the words from God's holy book come to you at particular times in your life. I couldn't tell you where they were found, but I could hear them vividly, *Therefore shall his calamity come suddenly; suddenly shall he be broken without remedy.* We both pulled the trigger at the same time. I felt a tug, the same shoulder, but he went down, a bullet in his darkened heart.

Looking around I saw the once white snow beginning to stain with the blood that once pumped life through the bodies. Five desperadoes lay dead; victims of the deed they sought to do. Checking the bodies I found that Wiggins was not among them, but there was a face I recognized—Curly Joe Dutton.

My gaze went up to the peaks. I was waiting, listening... Muncke had the men load the bodies in the wagons. I was to replace the guard on the wagon he was riding on. Toit was in no condition to be ridden.

I was in a solemn mood when the teamster barked at me, "Take off your coat. I want to take a looksee at your wound."

It brought me back to reality. I shrugged off my coat. It really didn't hurt, more of a burning sensation.

"Hmmm," I heard him. "Just graze with one bullet and looks like the other went through the fat of your arm. No real damage as long as you don't get lead poisonin'."

Reckon I'll add those scars to my collection. When the bodies were loaded, Muncke came by to check each wagon then we headed on down the pass.

It had begun to snow as we came off the pass and continued on into Durango. It was a light snow, soft, fluffy flakes. Muncke came by to check on me. "How're doin'?" he asked.

"Cold," came my reply with a shivver.

"I'll drop you off at the eatery then take Sanchez on over to the Doc's. He done gone unconscious on us. You get some coffee in your gullet and warm up. Me an' the boys will take care of the bodies and your horse."

I found a cup on the counter then moved toward the stove where there was a pot of coffee. Pouring a cup I set it on the table then began to struggle with my coat.

"Mister Forrest, there's blood all over your coat!" exclaimed Molly come out from the kitchen. "Let me help you get that coat off you so I can check that wound."

My arm hurt as we worked to get the coat off. My sleeve was soaked with blood. Molly flung her hand to her mouth in concern when Muncke came in the door then shooed her away.

"Molly, go make some fresh coffee and bring me a cup. My innards could use some warming." He then proceeded to remove my shirt and top of my longhandles.

"One of the boys is bringing the doc over as soon as he checks out Sanchez. I don't know what Tabor was seeing. You've got a graze and a hole through the fat of your arm, but there's another bullet in your shoulder," he informed me. I didn't recollect getting hit three times.

"Molly! Bring me a cloth and hot water!"

Benj was trying his best to clean off some of the blood and at the same time stop the bleeding from the two main wounds when the doctor came in.

"Hmmm, hmmm" the doc kept remarking over and over. "Mister Forrest, it seems like you have a couple of nice looking wounds. The bullet is just under the skin and that will be no problem cutting out. What's I'm worried about are the wounds themselves. I can't tell if there are pieces of your shirt in the wound or not. I'll flush it good, and do some probing."

Molly walked in with two cups of coffee. "Water is heating and I'll bring it... Miles!" she exclaimed dropping the cups.

"He's all right," assured the doctor. Then he surveyed the area. There was quite a bit of blood. "Molly, I'm sorry. I'll make sure it is all cleaned up."

She was visibly upset as she stooped down fumbling with the pieces of the broken cups. Standing I could see she was flushed, partly from being embarrassed from dropping the cups and partly from seeing all of the blood on and around me.

"I'll, I'll bring some more coffee," she muttered.

"Molly, bring the hot water first, if you don't mind. I need it to take care of these wounds," ordered the doctor.

He was just starting to cut the bullet out of the back of my shoulder when the door burst open. In walked the marshal.

CHAPTER 11

"You're under arrest for the murder of one, Sanfred Cutchins," he sneered. Wiggins was behind him wearing a large grin.

I pulled my pistol and held it under the table. Munke went over to head him off. "Marshal, what say we wander over to your office. Me and the boys want to swear an affidavit that will sure clear Miles of any wrong-doing."

"Won't do," he argued. "This man here said he saw Forrest shoot his friend."

I started to saw something, but Benj beat me to it. "That's an outright lie!" He put his hand to his gun in case Wiggins wanted to contest his statement. "That weasel wasn't there. If Cutchins is the man's name then he was part of a gang that tried to rob Mr. Kohlmeyer's wagons. He was shot dead along with the rest of the gang."

The marshal looked flustered, then turned his head to look at Wiggins. He started to turn away when Benj grabbed him by the shoulder. "If that weasel insists he was there then I want a warrant issued for his arrest for the murder of one of my men."

Wiggins had already started sneaking out toward the door. "No, no, I wasn't there." Then burst on out into the street.

The marshal took another couple of steps to follow when Benj got his attention again. "Marshal, you forgettin' something?" he asked pointing at me.

He sort of grunted something that sounded like an apology, tipped his hat then went on out.

"Jake, you stay here and help Forrest over to his room. I'm going to escort the marshal back to his office," he ordered, then gave me a little wave.

Doctor Farrington had pulled a few pieces of wool from my wounds and was in the process of sewing me up. When he finished he sort of jerked my arm around a bit, not too easily either, looking at his work. "Hmm, hmm, that'll do," he muttered, "unless there's a piece of cloth in there I didn't find, you should heal all right. I'll check on you tomorrow."

He picked up his equipment placing them in a black bag, pulled on his coat and left. Molly took a soft cloth and wiped off the excess blood from my shoulder.

When she finished, she went to the counter to get two cups then over to the stove to fill them with coffee. Coming back to me she sat down placing one cup in front of me.

"Mister Forrest..."

"Miles, Molly, it's Miles," I said with a smile.

"Scars, you're covered with scars," she said tearfully.

"There's a few," I replied but I thought if she could only see the hidden scars. "I guess that's how life is; scarred but still surviving."

A week later it finally hit; I woke to over two feet of snow. I went to the barn to check on Toit and then thought I'd head up town to see if people were stirring about. There was no traffic on the roads, but some of the shopkeepers were starting to clean off the boardwalks in front of their stores. I went over to the eatery and saw Molly struggling with a shovel, so I went over to help.

"Go on inside," I told her. "Make some coffee and I'll finish shoveling the walk off."

"But your shoulder," she protested.

"I'll be careful and it will be good for it," I replied reaching for the shovel. As I began work, I felt a little burning in my arm, but I had worse. I was careful enough not to tear the stitches out.

After I finished I went in and sat by the stove where Molly had placed a coffeepot. Looking around I decided that I surely liked this place. Molly came to fill a cup from the pot and set it in front of me then returned to the kitchen. In a minute or so she returned with a plate of elk chops, eggs, biscuits and gravy, along with a piece of custard pie on the side.

We were sitting there when the marshal walked in and came over to our table. I was sort of surprised he'd venture out and trudge through the snow. He didn't look too friendly, but when had he ever been friendly to me? He didn't seem too happy with Molly sitting there with me, but ignored her and glared at me.

"I've contacted the governor's office," he informed me. "This time you're not getting away with it. I've requested a special investigator to come from Denver to look into the murders."

I took a draught of coffee then wiped my moustache with the back of my hand. "What is it with you, marshal? As soon as you saw me you had it in for me. That ugly man stalked me for several weeks and he tried to steal the hard work of those miners."

He began to get red around the neck. "He killed one of the guards and came after me and now you accuse me of being a murderer when I was only doing my job! Seems that when a man does his job, protecting the work and life of others, he is the one who is accused."

"Go ahead with your investigation. I'm sure it will find that the bullet that killed the guard came from Ugly's gun. He was the only one carrying a .36. Go over and talk with his wife. How is she goin' to take care of three kids!" I stood up, not realizing that I had the fork that had been embedded in the gravy in my hand and pointed it at the marshal flinging gravy on his coat. "Don't you come botherin' me about killin' a piece of scum like him!"

In a fit of rage, he grabbed a chair, flung it across the room and stomped out. Molly was standing there observing with one hand covering her mouth and the other clenched by her side.

When I glanced at her I became ashamed. "I'm sorry. This shouldn't have happened in your place. What's the issue with the marshal anyhow?"

Picking up my cup she poured me another cup of coffee. "Sit down and eat your breakfast; it's getting cold." Then she went over to pick up the chair the marshal had thrown.

Coming back to me she placed the chair at the table where it belonged, then stood in front of me. "Marshal Garten likes to run the town and does not like anyone to stand up to him. Plus the fact that the man you killed was a distant cousin of a man who married his sister." Then she blushed, "He sort of assumes I am his property."

I stared her in the eyes until she could no longer hold my glance. "Are you?" I questioned.

"Miles, sit down and eat. There is, was, nothing. I have no feelings or thoughts regarding the Marshal," she answered placing her hand on my wounded shoulder. "But I am..." she stopped and hurried off to the kitchen.

I was just digging into my pie, glancing continually at the kitchen to see if Molly would come back out. My eyes were forced to the door as Muncke entered.

He picked up a cup from the counter before coming to the table. Stopping, he poured coffee, the addressed me. "Just bumped into the marshal. He said there is going to be a special investigation," he sipped his coffee then smiled. "Don't be worrying none, Wells Fargo and the miners will back us up."

CHAPTER 12

One thing about a Colorado snowstorm, especially in the fall of the year, when the sun came out the snow could quickly disappear. After the events of the past two weeks, I decided to take Toit out for a ride. He had enjoyed two weeks of rest, plus I wanted to get out of town and into God's great cathedral.

Riding along the Animas River I thought of Juanita. The last I had heard from her, she had been jilted and would be in Denver sometime in June. Her mother was doing well. Then the thoughts of Molly touching my shoulder and her delicious pie came to mind.

I stopped Toit at the edge of a stand of aspens and dismounted. I'm not one to practice a fast draw, but I did believe in practice, and also doing some shooting from time-to-time. I normally read my Bible in the morning and then for about fifteen minutes would work on my draw. The Schofield I always carried with me, but I also brought along my old .44. It doesn't get used much so figured I'd fire a few rounds from it. I liked it, but when Jim Albright introduced me to the Schofield on the trail to Dodge one time, I was sold. It felt a part of me; like an extension of my hand.

There is something about the wilderness, the mountains in particular. As I holstered my pistol I pulled out another weapon from my little arsenal and began to read Psalm 17. My life had seen plenty of death—through the War of the Rebellion, with McNelly and the Rangers, riding the trail, and working with Cook. It seemed like death and evil rode next to me at times.

I moved on to Psalm 18 and read verse 5, *The sorrows of hell compassed me about: the snares of death prevented me.* As I read on into verse 6 I felt a release, *In my distress I called upon the LORD, and cried unto my God: he heard my voice...* I could almost feel his smile as I looked up through the aspen to the sky marked by only a few clouds. The breeze moved on my face and I could hear the trickle of water under the ice of the river. The coolness of the air, the breeze and the ripping of the water seem to say to my soul, *Trust, Miles, simply trust.*

It was a good day. I dozed some lying on a rock near the river that had been warmed by the sun. When I mounted Toit, I sat for a moment breathing in the fresh, clean air, then I gave Toit a nudge and we headed back toward Durango.

Before heading back to stable Toit, I stopped at the eatery. The thought of pie nagged at me, and there was always coffee on the stove. A smile formed on my lips when I realized that there was now another reason.

Walking through the doorway I immediately saw Marshal Garten sitting in my spot by the stove. At least I had claimed it in my mind. I wanted to walk out but heard Muncke from a table to my right.

"Come on in, Miles. Let me introduce you to the governor's special investigator," he said in a mocking manner.

He got up from where he was sitting and took me over to the table where the marshal was sitting. *My table*, I thought.

"This here is Doc Shores."

I nodded. I knew Everett Shores. He was sheriff in Gunnison when I rode in that country. The other man seated had his back to me, yet something about him was familiar.

Doc acted as if he didn't know me. He didn't reach out to shake my head, just returned my nod. "You're Forrest?" he inquired. "Sit down, grab some coffee."

Molly had been standing near the entrance to the kitchen, and when I sat she brought me a cup of coffee. I almost choked on my first swallow when the other man spoke up.

He sneered and when he did I remembered who he was. "Forrest, I wouldn't be surprised if you're not involved in something crooked," he remarked then looked at Shores. "See, this man is known for his actions. He burned down my parent's house."

After I calmed myself, I replied, "It was war."

Molly walked over to refresh our cups. The man looked up at her. "Did you know he was married to my sister?" she seemed slightly startled by his pronouncement. "I tried to tell my mother and father that he was no good, but they wouldn't listen. Finally, when he joined the Union forces and then came to burn down the house around them, they understood what I had been talking about."

I sat there glowering and looking just over the rim of my cup. "Of course father already had the marriage annulled. Blythe stood there and watched our home burn to the ground, shivering and shaking," he announced then looked at Molly smiling.

The was a snicker from him at he turned his attention back to me. "Miles, you know there is more than one way to destroy a person."

He was beginning to perturb me, when bursting through the door came Kohlmeyer yelling, "The pass has been opened and I want to get a load on the road. Let's shake a leg!" Then turned walking out.

Muncke slapped me on the shoulder, "Let's go."

I gulped down the rest of my coffee, nodded at Molly when the voice called out, "Be seeing you." I didn't bother to turn.

It's been a week and the crew is just a few miles outside of Durango. The pass was open, but it took extra mules to pull the wagons through. All I could think of was that snake—Bently B. Brighton, by name.

I would never have thought I would ever see him again or hear anything about Blythe. My mind was pondering too much. A man can think more worries into his system before they actually take place. I thought I should say a few words to Molly, so after I left the wagon at the warehouse I walked over to the eatery.

As I walked through the door, I heard her scream. Brighton had hold of her and she was fighting to get away. He was holding her tight, trying to kiss her. My hand went to the Schofield, almost too easily. "Let her go!" I demanded.

There came a hideous laugh. It sounded like it was loosed from the gates of Hades. "No, Miles, this is just part of your payback."

I heard some sobbing and from the corner of my eye saw a woman with her apron up over the lower part of her face in the kitchen doorway. I didn't have time to dwell on her, my focus had to be Brighton.

"You always were a coward," I taunted. "You would hide behind your sister; always calling upon her to help you out of trouble." Hesitating before I continued to let the words work on him. "You said I burned your home. Bah! You never had a home. There wasn't an ounce of love between anyone in your family; it was all show. Now, let Molly go!"

"You won't shoot," he curled his lip in a contemptuous smile.

"You have to the count of three. One, two..." and on three I shot him in the shoulder knocking him back. Molly took the opportunity to escape from his clutches. "I surely can't have someone doubting my word."

"Send for the doctor," he pleaded. "Oh, my, I'm going to die."

I figured it wouldn't take long for the marshal to show up. Brighton was moaning, sitting at a table while I was with Molly at another. "This time you've gone too far. You shot a government man. Give me your gun, you're under arrest," proclaimed the marshal.

"You'll do no such thing, Marshal!" declared Molly. "I want Mr. Brighton arrested for assault. He was making advances on me and when Miles told him to let me go, he wouldn't. Miles shot him to protect my honor, and I fully intend to press charges against him."

Brighton was whimpering and writhing in his chair. Blubbering more about him dying. "Marshal, if I have to, I'll go get the mayor right now," Molly said, a little more indignant this time.

"Now, now," replied the marshal waving his hand at Molly. "No need to get yourself stirred up."

With that Molly stiffened. I thought she was going to explode, but she controlled herself. The marshal went over to help Brighton stand. As they were stumbling out, Molly called, "I'll be down shortly to file charges."

Then she looked at me, "I'll go get some coffee."

"You might want to check on the lady in the kitchen. She didn't look well," I informed her.

"Mother!" she exclaimed then hurried off to find her.

CHAPTER 13

I walked with Molly the next morning to the marshal's office. The sun wasn't shining and the day promised to be one of gloom and dreariness. I asked on the way over if she was sure she wanted to go through with this and she answered that she did. Upon arrival we found that Brighton wasn't there.

"Bail'd out," Garten grunted.

"By whom?" I wanted to know.

"Not your concern," he said not looking up from the papers on his desk.

I had a notion to swipe those papers off the desk, but there was already enough tension in the room that could be cut with a knife. Molly stomped a foot in frustration. "Give me the papers to sign my grievances."

He tossed them at her, never looking her direction. She quickly read over them before signing. "Come on, Miles," she said abruptly leaving the office.

We went over to the eatery where I reclaimed my customary seat by the stove. She went to the back and brought back some biscuits covered with white-eye gravy and a platter of fresh side. On the way to the marshal's she explained that her mother had just been startled but was doing fine now.

She filled cups of coffee for the both of us. "All right, Miles, talk," she said as she sat down next to me.

I deliberately took a mouthful of the delight that was in front of me as I was hesitant to say anything. Molly reached out and pulled my plate away. "Talk."

Swallowing the biscuit and gravy that I had in my mouth I began to tell her of my two-day marriage to Blythe and my joining the Union army. The Brighton plantation was right on the boundary of Virginia and the newly formed West Virginia where I lived.

My unit, under Captain Kidd was chasing a band of Mosby's raiders and was ordered to burn any plantation that might be able to aid the Confederate forces. It was deemed to be my duty to torch the Brighton plantation. Then I told her that when my unit freed the slaves that Blythe and her father spit on me.

"Miles, I'm surprised you even married her. "Didn't you realize that your beliefs were miles apart? Was she even a believer?"

"Never thought about it much back then. She, along with her parents attended an Anglican Church. They didn't much approve of my Baptist persuasion," I replied then helped myself to another bite.

After taking a swallow of coffee to help wash down the biscuit I continued more softly. "Young love —foolish love. The Lord intervened in a strange way."

"What about the scars? It shocked me when I saw so many. Tell me Miles, I'd like to know."

Without going into detail I mentioned the war, then riding with McNelly's Rangers, the trips up the trail and some other events. I mentioned the ordeal of the winter I stayed and helped Juanita and her mother.

She sipped her coffee, then quietly asked, "What about Juanita?"

Pondering on how to answer there came a scream from the kitchen. We rushed in, the kitchen was aflame along with her mother's apron and dress. I rushed to her taking her outside and covered her with snow and water from the puddles telling her to lie down in them.

Rushing back in I saw Molly trying to fight the fire, but immediately saw that the building was doomed. When I grabbed her she pulled away from me to continue to fight the flames. I had to pick her up and carry her outside. The danger now was that the fire would go to the surrounding buildings. Durango, at that time had no fire department.

"Molly go warn those in the other buildings!"

She dashed to the other stores. I stood there looking at the flames now consuming the eatery and beginning to lick at the adjacent building. Sighing I went to Molly's mother and lifted her up. She had burns on her arm, but not blistered except one on the back of her left hand. I reckoned the snow and cold water might have helped.

It didn't take long for the town folk to show up; a fire is always an attraction. Fortunately there were only three buildings on that block and they were soon consumed. Molly came to join her mother and stood beside me. I was pleasantly surprised as I felt her take my hand.

I looked at her watching the blaze; there was a peace in her countenance. Turning back to look at the fire, the scene took me back to the war...to the burning of the Brighton plantation. It seemed as the flames whipped around devouring the wooden structures that I could imagine the devil grinning at me.

Her mother began to sob, then to outright cry. Molly reached for her and enfolded her in her arms holding her tight.

"I, I don't know how the fire started," her mother sobbed. "It wasn't from the stove, it was at the back door."

We stood for a while along with the rest of the town looking at the blackened ruins wrought by the fire. I saw Doc Shores standing by the marshal and excused myself from Molly to go have a little chat with them. On my way there I saw Dr. Farrington and pointed him toward Molly and her mother.

"Are you goin' to issue a warrant?" I asked the marshal.

"What warrant?" he answered in surprise.

"Brighton's. You know he did this?"

Anger began to show on his face. "There is no proof of that! Because you have a personal grudge against him is not reason to accuse him, besides he's a federal agent direct from Washington!" he barked.

"Marshal, anyone at Molly's that night heard him. He brought up the fire at his plantation, a few days later he mauled Molly. Anyone with any sense knows he did it!"

He turned and walked away. Gritting my teeth I glanced at Doc Shores then turned to walk back to Molly and her mother. Fortunately they had a little place a couple of blocks from the eatery so I escorted them home to settle them in. The doctor informed me that her burns were not bad, and that he would come by tomorrow to check on the only bad one on the back of her hand.

As we were walking I heard a movement. Swiftly my gun was in my hand.

"Little jumpy aren't you, Forrest?" It was Doc Shores. "Just wanted to let you know that you and the guard crew are in the clear. It was all part of the job and in self-defense. Mind if I tag along with you for a while?"

Neither of us answered so he took that as a "yes." We walked along in silence to the house; Molly's mother went on inside. Doc asked if he could talk with us for a minute. "I'm truly sorry for what happened. May I ask what your plans might be?"

"Doc," I began but Molly touched my arm.

"It's all right. Mr. Shores, I'll start looking for a place to rebuild. Everything's gone and first thing to do is look for a place. Have to replace the stove, dishes, silverware—everything. I'm not sure how much we can afford, and I don't know where a stove can be found."

Deep inside my soul I kept hearing, *Trust, Trust.* "Molly," I interrupted. "I have a little money and would sure like the opportunity to be a business partner with you. I only have one condition—pie will be on the house."

She smiled, grasping my arm, "Miles, I can't let you give me money."

"I wouldn't be giving it. I would be investing."

"Let me help," came the concerned voice of Doc Shores. "You write what you would like in a stove. I'll shop around Denver to find a good one to your liking," he said sort of hesitantly. "Miles, Dave Cook took the initiative to deposit some money into your account in Denver. It seems that Cooke Brown had money on his head."

I didn't say anything, just frowned at what he told me. I wasn't one to take money for the killing of anyone, including an outlaw.

"Molly, I'll be leaving in a couple of days. If you could give me directions I'd appreciate it." He tipped his hat to Molly then walked away.

"I'll take tomorrow off. Kohlmeyer wants me to make a run to Silverton. There are some tools and other equipment he wants me to pick up. I'll be gone about a week, but I don't have to leave immediately," I informed her. "You'll not walk out after dark, and be sure and carry a weapon with you. Despite what the marshal says, Brighton is behind this."

"You giving me orders now, Mr. Forrest?" she asked sternly. "Just because you're an investor doesn't give you the right to boss me around."

I stiffened at the rebuke. "I'm just a-sayin', well, 'cause I care for you," I stuttered which now brought a laugh.

"My, my," she said. "Don't you stutter when you get flustered." And she laughed some more. It was nice to hear despite the recent tragedy.

CHAPTER 14

As I drove the team up to Kohlmeyer's warehouse in Silverton, there was a man standing by the loading docks. When I stepped from the wagon, he walked over to greet me.

Thrusting out his hand, "Name's Johnson. I heard about the fire. Is Helen and Molly all right?"

I shook his hand, but he must have understood my puzzled look. "Sorry, Frank Johnson. Helen is my wife and Molly my daughter."

It seemed strange that he would be up here in Silverton while his family was in Durango, but then again many miners worked away from family. Knowing the vice in Silverton, I could understand him wanting to keep the women away.

The men hurried to unload the wagon then load it with the tools and equipment I was to take back that needed repair.

"Mister Johnson, the ladies are doin' fine. Your wife has a burn on the back of one hand," I replied.

He was rubbing his whiskered chin wanting to say more, but finally all that came out was, "You tell Helen and Molly that I'll be down at the end of next week if the passes don't close." Then he walked away before I could say anything more.

I went on down to the cafe next to the hotel to grab a bite to eat. By the time I was finished, they would have the wagon loaded and a fresh team hitched so I could be on my way.

On my way back I stopped in a little grocery to purchase a few things: bacon and coffee primarily. I looked at the shelf and saw that they had beans in a can. What next? I wondered, but asked for a couple of cans along with some canned peaches.

As I headed back to Durango, I tried not to think too much about the fire. I wanted to push it into the back of my mind where I hoarded a bunch of other junk that I'd collected through the years. I knew Brighton was behind it.

Molly's father acted a bit strange and surely seemed as if he didn't want to talk with me much. At least now I knew their last name, and I wouldn't have to go around saying, "Molly's mother," when I referred to her. I pondered that as well. Why wasn't I told their names?

About a third of the way down the pass it happened. I heard the explosion above me and looked up. Snow was beginning to cascade down the mountain—avalanche. I tried to whip the mules into action but saw that was no use. Grabbing the Greener and my poke of goods I jumped off and started running back up the road. Slipping and falling in the snow and mud I saw a ledge. The avalanche hit the wagon; I heard the mules screaming as I dove under the ledge. The snow may cover me, but at least I knew which way was up when I began to dig out.

It was only minutes until the roar was over. I how no idea how much snow was on top of me. It was dark under the ledge but I knew which way to start moving. I removed the shells from the shotgun and using the stock for a shovel began to slowly dig out at an angle.

As I was working I thought, *Miles, old boy, you sure do get yourself into some predicaments.* As I dug I could see that the snow was lighter, so I pushed the Greener through opening up a hole to the outside. I began to crawl and slide up out of my little cave. Exiting, the brightness blinded me. The sun was glaring off the surface of the snow. There was no sign of the wagon or mules. I hated the thought of the way those animals had died.

Looking around to get my bearings I slowly started out. It was hard going through the snow and I wanted to stay as close as I could to the mountain side. I began to tire as I put a leg forward then pulled the other out. I was up to my hips in snow. I didn't know how far the avalanche covered the road, but I hoped it stopped down around the bend. That would be about a quarter mile. It took a spell; walking in almost waist deep snow wears a fellow out, but slowly and surely I made it.

I looked up to try and figure out what time it was. I needed to hurry if I wanted to get down off the pass by nightfall and make camp. Stopping for a moment I thanked the Lord for His protection, and it was only then that I remembered that my one hand clenched on to my supplies. I would count it a feast when I settled in. I could have easily been buried under that snow along with the mules and wagon.

Moving down to the bottom of the pass I stepped off the road a few yards to build a fire. After getting a blaze going I searched around for wood so I could keep it going all night. It would be getting cold and I didn't have my bedroll with me.

I wasn't very careful that night as I kept the fire blazing. My sheepskin coat kept my body warm that day but my feet were nigh to being froze from walking in the snow, slush, and mud. Hopefully tomorrow I could make it down to Hermosa. There were a few small ranches there.

It was right at suppertime when I arrived back in Durango the next day. I sure came riding in with style—on a sway back old mule that I was able to secure from one of the ranches. But, say, it sure did beat walking. As I came into town I saw Molly in front of the destroyed eatery talking with the marshal. I pulled up in front of them. Maybe it's just the way my mind works, but I thought I saw surprise in the marshal's eyes.

"Miles!" she exclaimed and looked at me sitting on top of that old mule. "Where's the wagon?"

I ignored the question for I was rankled some that she was with the marshal. "Your father said he would be down at the end of the week if he could."

She smiled and said, "There won't be much for him to do. There was almost nothing left, though Bull, uh, Marshal Garten has been helpful."

Now that rankled me even more, perhaps to the point of agitation.

"He's been so kind," she continued. We went through the rubble and most of it is rubbish, not fit to be using again. The old stove that set in the eatery seems to be all right; that's about all we salvaged."

"I heard there was an avalanche," ventured the marshal.

"That so?" I queried raising my eyebrows.

"Couple of miners heading up the pass almost got caught, had to turn back. I'm surprised you made it through. They said the pass might be closed for several weeks from the look of things," he remarked with what I thought was too glib of tongue.

I didn't bother to tell him how I made it through the pass; just stared at him and said, "Well, a person just doesn't know how the good Lord will work."

"I was on my way home, you're welcome to come by for a bite to eat. I'm sure momma would welcome you," Molly remarked.

Declining her offer I said I would drop by sometime tomorrow. "I need to let Kohlmeyer know I'm back," I said making an excuse. "And to let him know about his wagon and mules."

She looked somewhat disappointed, but I wanted to get away from Marshal Garten. "Fine, I want you to help me look for a new location tomorrow."

"Oh! I just remembered an appointment!" exclaimed the marshal. "I'm sorry Molly, I have to leave," and he turned on his heel to walk away.

"That's sudden-like," she said to no one in particular.

"Until tomorrow," I said tipping my hat. Kicking the mule a little harder than I should have, we moved on down to the livery.

I slid off the mule tying it to a post out front. Silas Gibson must have been watching from the little window on his shack for he came out struggling to put on a coat.

"Fine specimen of animal yuh got there, Forrest," he said laughing.

Giving him a disgusted look, I simply said, "I don't need any lip from you, Gibby. Just put him away for me."

He laughed again, then went over to pull open the large door to lead the mule into the stable. No matter what kind of animal, mule or horse, I knew Gibby would take care of it.

I was still standing there when he came back out a few minutes later. "Rubbed him down a bit, I'll go back later and finish. He's got found. Come on in, there's coffee on the stove and yuh can tell me how yur ridin' an ol' mule."

"Thanks," I said rubbing down the side of my face. "I have something I need to check on. I'll tell you my story later."

I walked off to see if I could find the marshal. There was something nagging at me, and I wanted to see where he went. I didn't quite believe his story of the miners telling him about the avalanche.

CHAPTER 15

I didn't know where to start looking for the marshal, so I put that thought aside and walked down toward Kohlmeyer's warehouse and office. It wasn't far with only a feed store separating Gibby's livery from that of Kohlmeyer's.

It was nearly the last of twilight as I passed by the Kohlmeyer livery. I thought I heard the sound of voices. It could be a couple of the teamsters, but Barney, the hostler, should have been in the sack as he has to be up early.

With my inquisitive nature, I just had to check it out. In a few more minutes it would be dark. I tried to be nonchalant as I approached the door which was slightly opened. Edging through, over in the corner with a lantern were two men—Marshal Garten and Brighton. I moved a little closer when I felt a gun placed to the back of my neck.

"Well, lookee here," the cackling voice said. It was that little weasel Wiggins. "Keep a-walkin' Mr. Forrest. Lookee here, Marshal, at what I found sneakin' 'round."

Brighton, with his arm in a sling, struggled some to pull out his gun while the marshal already has his out and ready. "You were supposed to die in that avalanche," said the marshal.

I saw Brighton's lips curl as he snarled, "I've waited a long time for this." He took a step toward me then lifted his gun.

Wiggins had forgotten to take my guns, weak-mined as he was. The Greener was hidden by my coat. I pulled it up firing one barrel taking Brighton down. The shot startled Wiggins forcing him to take a step back. He discharged his gun, but fortunately for me he stumbled firing into the air. Whirling I pulled the trigger emptying the other barrel into Wiggins.

It was then I felt the pain in my left side. Once, then again. Dropping the shotgun, I pulled my pistol firing at the marshal and saw him stumble. He fired a third shot at me. Brighton was now struggling to sit up. The shot hit his arm and side, and I could see that he was bleeding from his face.

I was laying on my side trying to raise my gun watching the marshal shuffle toward me. I forgot about Brighton as I tried to bring my gun to bear on the marshal as his pistol stared me down. I fired and the marshal fell to the ground, then another shot. Looking to the side I saw a pair of black boots.

There was the sound of footsteps running. "Miles, you didn't have to kill him!" came the voice of Molly whose was now standing next to the man with the black boots.

I was losing blood and consciousness. A slight smile came across my face and I thought, *well, you ol' fence post, you really did it this time.*

When I came to the first thing I realized was that I wasn't lying in the dirt of Kohlmeyer's stable. I was thirsty, and I didn't know if anyone was around, but I hollered, "I sure could use a cup of coffee!"

"Molly!" a voice yelled. "Get a cup of coffee for this lazy hombre. Maybe a glass of water too. 'Bout time you decided to wake up, you lazy sluggard."

The voice seemed familiar. I shook my head a few times to try and remove the cobwebs that seemed to fill my brain. The man talking looked like Doc Shores, but, I shook my head again, he was supposed to be in Denver.

"The coffee's hot, so take a swallow of this water first," came the voice of Molly as she held the glass to my lips. I was afraid to look her in the face as I remembered the last words I heard from her. She thought I had killed the marshal...what was his name? My mind was still hazy.

My hand went out for the coffee that she had set on the stand by the bed; that's when the pain hit me like a sledgehammer in the side. As she picked up the cup when she saw me trying to get it, my hand hit hers knocking the cup to the floor spilling the coffee. All I could think of was, *now you've really done it,* and lost unconsciousness.

I felt like I was on fire. Whew, if this is what Hades feels like, I want no part of it. I heard screaming and cursing. My eyes were barely open and there was a dark man holding a black horse with another one of greenish hue next to it. There were blood streaks on the horses, as if they had been raked deep and rode hard.

When I tried to sit up, the pain in my side struck me like a fiery sword. It took all my will to keep from passing out. The man standing by the greenish horse was yelling and I could see the spittle flying from his mouth as he cursed. I couldn't see who he was screaming at, but there were no words or movement from the direction in which he was looking.

He turned and approached the place where I was lying. A dark, eerie, foreboding feeling came over me. My innards were churning and it seemed my fever was intensifying. It was dark all around, so dark it could be felt; dark, all except one spot of light.

I saw a hand stretch out of the light. Immediately the two horses and their riders were gone. A hand touched the side of my face.

"Doctor! He's awake!" a voice exclaimed. My hand reached for the cool, soft hand on my cheek. Through half-opened eyes I saw—it was Molly.

CHAPTER 16

I had been cooped up in a room, I assumed in Molly's house, for several weeks, the first of which I had to stay in bed. I was in and out of consciousness the first day, being weak from loss of blood.

The second day Doc Farrington and Molly were in the room checking on my wound. Molly said the snow had stopped, but it was still cold as she stoked the fire in the little stove that was in the room and added more wood.

"We thought that you might not make it," said the Doc looking at me with a scowl. "That being said, I am worried. One bullet passed on through, but the other two are still in your body and I'm afraid to probe for them. You've lost enough blood."

Molly came over to the bedside taking me by the hand. The doctor continued with his prognosis. "Those bullets can move and eventually rupture a vital, however, operation is out of the question."

I saw the concern on his face as he took off the bandages and began to clean the wound. As he wiped around one of the wounds his eyes opened wide. "This cannot be!" he exclaimed. "It's impossible!" He reached for his bag pulling out scissors to clip the sutures then went back to his bag for forceps. I groaned a little as he pulled, emerging with a bullet. It was partially out of the wound.

He went to business cleaning up the wound and stitching it tighter. The flesh around the wound was now tender and I clenched tightly on Molly's hand as he sewed. He kept muttering, "Impossible, impossible."

After that chore was finished he went to check the wound on my back. "Good, good," he muttered, "but, but what's this?" He felt across my back and inside my skin was a hard lump.

Without saying anything he went back to his black bag pulling out a scapel. "Hold tight, I'm going to cut."

He sliced through the skin and out popped the other bullet. Picking it up he just began to shake his head.

"Guess the good Lord did a little surgery on me," I said in a whisper.

Standing he went over to the basin to wash his hands. "Impossible," he kept muttering. "This can have happened."

Molly was staring, eyes wide open. "Miles, how?"

"I'm not really sure," I said in weakened voice. "I was having a fitful dream, but it seemed real, and in it the Lord told me it wasn't time yet, and I saw a hand coming from a light."

I was getting sleepy from the ordeal and could barely keep my eyes open, but I needed to explain. "Molly, I'm sorry about..."

That was as far as I got before she began to shush me. "Doc Shores told me that he killed both the marshal and Brighton. And just for your ignorant mind, the marshal was just helping me. He was an acquaintance only. So don't jump to conclusions without the facts, buster."

I think I gave a half-smile.

It was a week before I could hobble up and down the hall and back. However, I was determined to make it to the supper table instead of eating in bed. I was anxious to be up and around. Kohlmeyer came around to see me a couple of times informing me that he would give me half wages until I could get back on the job.

I wanted to get out and check on Toit. He would be wondering where I was. However, whenever Molly would see me up out of bed, I would catch it from her. It was a blessing that she was there to care for me, but it was becoming a nuisance.

Finally, at the end of the third week, when neither Molly or her mother were around I dressed myself, grabbed a coat and went outside. If felt delicious—the fresh air was invigorating and the sunshine warmed my face. I was walking toward the stable when I was accosted by Kohlmeyer who asked if I could sit a wagon seat. The pass was open and they needed supplies. I was still a mite sore, but not hurting severely, so I told him I could make the delivery as long as I didn't have to load or unload.

That night at supper I could sense the tension at the table. No one said anything, no one looked at each other. Then Molly with a stern look on her face slapped his hands down on the table. "Absolutely not!" she declared. "How dare he even consider you driving a team!"

After some coaxing and compromising she relented on the condition that she and her mother be allowed to come on the trip. With the last snow and the avalanche her father had not been able to make his promised trip. Both of them demanded that they go with me. Now, I had learned from Juanita and Isabella that you just cannot argue with a woman that determined.

Kohlmeyer reluctantly agreed that they could travel with me. The first part of the trip wasn't bad, but by the end of the day my side was becoming me a mite painful. I was beginning to think I shouldn't have made the trip, but felt I couldn't let Kohlmeyer down. The rest of the crew had gone up the day before, and I was carrying up a wagon full of sugar, flour, and coffee. When we stopped for the night, the women had to help me down from the wagon, and I felt like, well, like an old woman.

Neither of them said anything, but I knew they were thinking "I told you so." Molly went scrounging for wood while I sat on the ground and got the fire started. Then I began to prepared the sleeping quarters. I dropped a canvas from the wagon as a backdrop and then another over the top to make a lean-to. That would give them plenty of privacy.

It just about did me in. I ate a few beans that Mrs. Johnson had prepared and chewed on some bacon, but then fell into my soogan and slept. Slept too soundly, for I didn't waken until I smelled the coffee the next morning. It bothered me some that I didn't wake up—dangerous thing to do on the trail.

We had coffee, bacon, refried beans, and Mrs. Johnson had even made biscuits. I felt somewhat refreshed but as soon as I tried to lumber aboard the wagon I felt a twinge in my side.

It was muddy and there was quite a bit of water running from the melting snow as the temperature had warmed up some. We were going a little slower than I had hoped. That was good in one way as it helped my side some, the slower pace, but bad that we would be on the road another day.

I didn't feel much better the next night when we stopped. That night the women-folk were plenty tired as well. I actually stopped a little early so we could have a decent meal for supper. It is much better when traveling to eat something good and filling, especially when going up into the high country.

While the ladies were preparing supper, I wandered down to a little stream caused by the runoff. As I was standing there my mind started to wander. Molly came up behind me and scared me nigh to death. That was twice I didn't hear anything. I felt that the Lord had told me to stay alert, and here I was neglecting that advice. I would wind up a victim for the forces of evil out there if I kept that up. The stream was rushing fairly rapidly so I used that as an excuse not to hear her.

"It's beautiful here," she said.

I surely couldn't disagree. The mountains were still blanketed with snow and the evergreens stood out against the white. The water cascaded down over the rocks, splashing up here and there.

"Molly, look at that water. It looks refreshing, but it is so cold it would make the bones ache. It looks as if a person could get in it and go right on down to the Animas and on to Durango. Kinda like life. Looks like it should be an easy journey, but just like the river there are obstacles. Rocks lay just under the surface that could smash a person, and just downstream, out of sight is a small rapid that could throw a person under and possibly bring death. Yep, life is like a river."

"Why, Miles, you are quite the philosopher," she said smiling.

"A person who has ridden as many miles as I have gets to ponderin' quite a bit. Yuh never know what I might come up with." I looked at her and she blushed.

Her mother had been cutting some potatoes and had some beef cut into cubes simmering in a pot over the fire. I glanced down and was tempted to peek at the Dutch oven.

"You stay away from that Miles Forrest," warned Mrs. Johnson, "or you won't get any."

While we were waiting for the stew, I wanted Molly to check my wounds while the sun was still shining and she could see. She cleaned them off, one was oozing a little blood, and put on clean bandages.

"More wounds to add to your collection," she sighed as she wrapped me up again. "Oh, Miles..."

That night we enjoyed the stew and Mrs. Johnson, I was told outright to call her Helen, revealed the surprise in the Dutch oven—peach cobbler.

"Ma'am, now that is a real treat on the trail."

She frowned, "Helen is my name."

"Mighty tasty. Yuh know the Lord is just like that. When the way and the goin' gets rough at time He often gives us a little treat just like that peach cobbler." I looked at Molly smiling, "There I go philosophyzing again."

CHAPTER 17

Due to the melting snow, the roads were a slushy, muddy mess; we had to stop for a third night. It wasn't something I wanted to do, but with the conditions and my side there was no other choice. I sighed deeply as I stepped off the wagon seat, holding on tightly and looking over the mules toward the place I had chosen for the night. I knew from experience the obstacles and quirks that you might find along the trail, or maybe I should say, might find you.

By this time we all knew our camp chores. I was busy getting a fire started, Molly was gathering wood, and Helen was fixing up their sleeping quarters. I told her to cut some of the spruce boughs so they wouldn't have to lie on the wet ground.

It was a simple, but good supper of bacon and biscuits. The coffee was hot and strong, and sure hit the spot, especially now that the temperature was dropping in the twilight.

I heard some noise, looked for the Greener and saw it up in the wagon bench. I took the loop off the hammer of my pistol when a voice sounded out.

"Hey, the camp! Alright to come in?"

At least the man showed his trail manners. I was always suspicious of a fellow drifting so late and not setting up camp, but then I had to remind myself of the many times that I had done the same thing.

He rode in and started to dismount when he saw my hand on the butt of my gun. He straightened back up in the saddle looking at me. "Mind if I dismount?"

I nodded my head watching him all the time. He was wary, dismounting away from me placing his horse between us. He tied the horse to the back of the wagon, and I motioned with my head to the fire.

"Help yurself to some coffee, bacon's done et up, but thar's a couple of biscuits left." Molly looked at me a little strangely as I was pouring on the loose grammar and slang. She stood then went to the wagon for a clean cup.

"I was going to travel a little further before I stopped then smelled the woodsmoke. Nice to have some company on the trail I always say," he informed us not looking at me, but at Molly.

He wasn't a miner; I could easily see that by his clothes and the fine horse he was riding. Was I just being overly cautious? Nah, a person can't be too careful in this part of the country.

Molly brought the cup and poured him some coffee. Helen went about doing little chores, glancing at him then at me every once in a while. Molly walked off down toward the little creek while I went to the wagon for my bedroll. Helen had cut enough boughs for a pallet for me. When I turned back from the wagon, I saw that the stranger was not around.

I glanced quickly toward the wagon bench where I had placed the shotgun. I had told the women never to leave camp without taking it with them. It was my hope that it was with Molly.

Concern was growing in my mind. He was gone and Molly hadn't returned from the stream. I went looking for either one. Just before reaching the stream, I saw the man peering through the bushes.

"Why, you slimy..." He turned and I hit him, then again, and again. He staggered back. I wasn't about to give up my advantage. I drew my gun.

"Miles, no!" Molly shouted. I turned in her direction. Mistake. He picked up a branch swinging it at me where it connected with my wounded side. I doubled over and almost dropped from the blow and pain. He perceived something was wrong so he hit me there again. This time I dropped to the ground losing grip on the pistol and holding my side. He came over to kick me in the side smashing my fingers as I tried to protect my wound. A second kick, I was in terrible pain, ready to pass out when I heard the blast of the shotgun.

"Back off mister!" came the stern voice of Molly. "No, just back off, don't step in any other direction. There's one more barrel and I'm not wanting to use it, but I will."

I started gaining my senses even though my side was hurting something fierce. Seeing my gun I sort of half-scooted, half-crawled to where it was. Picking it up I came to my knees and tried to stand. "Molly, I need your help."

She saw that I had my gun pointed at the man so she lowered hers and rush to help me stand. "Git," I said through clenched teeth. The man stood there. I raised my gun pulling back the hammer. "Git on yur hoss and ride. Yu'll not be a-stayin' in this camp tonight."

He moved back toward the camp with me following him. Molly had moved off to the side so if she had to shoot, the mules and her mother would not be in line with her fire.

The man moved slowly and untied his horse. After he saddled up he looked at me. "This is not the last time we'll meet," he warned then put a spur to his horse.

It was time for my bravado to give out and I slumped to the ground. Molly rushed to help take off my shirt to check my wounds. The bandage was bloody as I had taken a couple of good licks from that branch and a kick. I thought that perhaps a rib was broke. Most likely, I thought, right between the bullet holes.

"Momma, help me get him to the fire, then heat up some water." Within minutes she had cleaned up the bleeding which was only superficial, but my side was throbbing.

I groaned, "Help me to my bedroll." When I reached it I collapsed. I couldn't get inside it so Molly helped me to lay on top of it then covered me with the blanket we kept on the wagon seat. I looked at the women and smiled.

The next morning it took real effort for me to get to my feet and totter over to the fire where Helen had coffee brewing. After coffee and bacon the women cleaned up camp and I looked at the daunting task of trying to climb up on the wagon bench.

It took time, both ladies had to help—one pushing, the other pulling. It wasn't a pretty sight. The sweat was pouring off my face even though the morning was cool. I was holding on tight trying not to pass out.

"Ever drive a team?" I asked looking at Molly. She shook her head no. "Well, you are today."

I handed her the reins and sat there slumped over while Helen fashioned a pallet just behind the seat on top of the supplies. "Just keep some tension on the reins. Don't ride the brake, but if you think you need to stop, don't hesitate. We're only a few hours away. I can help if something serious doesn't come up."

It was now two days later that I was lying on a cot in the back of Kohlmeyer's make-shift store. A fever never came on, but I sure was helpless. We figured a couple of ribs had been broken, but at least my wounds hadn't opened up. It was downright embarrassing to be helped to do everything, including shuffling to the privy. I barely remembered being carried from the wagon.

It was about midmorning of that day when the explosion came. It nigh shook me off the cot. Soon I could hear the commotion of folk running and a man bursting into the store.

"Johnson!" came the cry. "Come on! There's been an explosion and cave in at the Lucky Lenora. We need every man."

He ran out, followed by Molly and her mother. I tried to get out of bed. I reached for my boot when what felt like an axe-handle smashed against my side.

"Feel good, tough man?" came the ugly voice.

"Told you I would see you again," he snarled. "No one tells Ben Cagle to leave a camp." He swung the handle connecting with my shoulder and I toppled to the floor.

He must have come in through the back during the commotion of the explosion and the men running out to the mine.

As he was raising the handle to strike again Molly came in. "Miles!"

He turned to look at her giving me the chance to lunge for my pistol hanging on the edge of the cot. I shot, missed. As he swung the club at me, Molly shoved a chair toward him stopping the blow from landing and throwing him off balance. I fired again this time hitting him underneath the left arm knocking him back. I could feel the sweat dripping off my face as I was struggling to maintain consciousness; the pain in my side was something fierce.

I saw Molly gasp throwing her hands to her face. The man called Cagle moaned then tried to scream. "Miles, who is that?"

"He called himself Ben Cagle. He's the guy we ran out of camp."

"No, no, the other man," she was almost in hysteria. "When Cagle saw him he tried to scream. He came in and drug the body out, but, but, it's still there. Oh, Miles, I'm going insane," she cried sitting down on the edge of the cot next to me.

I took her in my arms, holding her despite the pain in my side. I hadn't seen anyone enter and the body was lying next to the chair bleeding all over the floor.

"Breathe deep, Molly," I instructed her. I knew who or what she saw. "You're all right. That was Death comin' to gather the soul to take it to judgment. I've seen the foul thing a few times, and no, you're not goin' insane," I told her, pulling her tighter. "He is a fearful thing."

I could see that she was gathering her wits. She leaned back from my embrace to look at me, then Cagle's body on the floor, then back at me. Without saying anything she moved away, got up, and left the room.

Here I was, in sincere, honest-to-goodness pain. A man had come trying to beat the living daylights out of me. I shot him and she ups and leaves him on the floor and me sitting here. I started to try to move around on the cot...

CHAPTER 18

The next morning I woke early. Feeling much better except for the ache in my side I set out to clean my guns. I noticed that while I was sleeping or unconscious, whichever it was, Cagle's body had been taken out of the room. I heard movement in the other room; into the backroom where I had been lying came a group of men.

I almost felt alarmed, sitting there with my pistol taken apart. Out of habit I looked for the Greener which was standing back against the wall. My fears were false; it seems that the men were sort of a peace commission for the mining camp.

"Forrest, you just seemed to have gotten in the way. This here Cagle was a vindictive man, had a problem with people he felt wronged him. He was here to kill Crach Talog, the foreman at the Lucky LeNora. Seems they had a history that started back in Leadville. He swore that he would get Talog one day. We figured it was him that dynamited the mine," concluded the speaker of the commission.

Another man added, "Good thing he didn't know much about explosives."

A third man piped in, "Only two were injured, and no one killed. We were able to get it cleared enough to get the men out in an hour. Crach identified Cagle as the same man in Leadville. Seems like he had to leave there on a fast horse."

"Most likely there's a wanted poster on him," remarked the second man. "Be sure to check when you get back down to Durango."

From the back a voice spoke in heavy Welsh accent, "I be thankin', you Forrest. Now I don't have to worry 'bout him any more." The man pushed through the others reaching out his hand to shake mine. He had a hard calloused hand with a firm grip.

I didn't say anything, just nodded. The men turned and left. I heaved a sigh and went back to cleaning my guns. While I was in the process of putting my guns away and cleaning up Molly came in with a cup of coffee.

She had been watching me and had a concerned look on her face. I looked at her as she set the cup down and her eyes bore into mine. "Miles, how many men have you killed?" Nervously she was tapping her fingers on the edge of the table. "I've known you only a short time and you've killed several. Do you like it? Doesn't it bother you?"

Taking the cup, I took a tentative sip to check how hot it was, then a deep swallow to put my thoughts together before I answered.

"Do I like it—No. Does it bother me—Yes," I said curtly. "For some reason I have a talent..."

She cut me off. "Killing is not a talent!"

I took another sip waiting for her to calm before I answered. "Years ago, Captain McNelly taught me a great lesson. God gave people different talents. Some are good with horses, others are fine carpenters...I happen to be good with a gun."

She started to interrupt when I raised my hand. "Molly, I have never used them in anger, for vengeance, or personal vendetta. They have only been used in defense of myself or others. As some may be called to the pulpit, to the field of medicine, McNelly told me that others, like myself are called to justice."

"You're a bloody man," she said in a whisper.

Looking at her with weary eyes I replied, "So was David. And I have to face the consequences just like he did. Often, all too often, I see the devil grinning at me."

I dropped my head looking in a half-empty cup of coffee. The silence was deafening in the room. Lifting my head and focusing on her again. "I don't go lookin' for trouble. Molly, I really don't."

She held my gaze for a few seconds. "Miles, the Commandment says, 'thou shalt not kill.'"

My eyes locked on hers as I holstered my pistol and asked, "Who will protect the innocent? Who will take care of the weak? Who will bring the wicked to justice?" I asked then paused waiting for the words to sink in before I continued.

"The Lord has seemed to have put me often in that position. I don't relish it; I didn't ask for it, but I will not run from it. Think, what would have happened to you and your mother in that camp with Cagle?"

She lingered another few seconds then turned to leave me alone. I sat at the little table for a few minutes with my thoughts. Thoughts that have run through my mind several times over the years. Thoughts that I have often questioned and once in a while tried to run away from. Then down deep in my souls, I heard, *your steps are ordered by Me.*

I cleaned myself up, well, at least the best I could. The wounds were a little sore and I groaned a few times if I moved the wrong way. However, my stomach was giving me fits and I reckoned I could walk down to the eatery.

Helen and her husband, Mr. Johnson, were in heavy conversation when I came from the back of the store. When they saw me they went silent. I nodded at them, and Johnson took a step my direction.

"How yuh feelin'?" he inquired. "Think yuh can drive it back to Durango? Sky's clear, but that's not promised for long this time of year."

Touching my side, I answered that I could make it, then mentioned that I was going down to get something to eat.

"Wagon's loaded, would yuh mind takin' Mrs. Johnson back, she won't be stayin'?"

I glanced at her and when our eyes met she turned her head. I don't think she was much happy with Mr. Johnson.

I didn't hurry through breakfast and made sure that I had my fill. We would most likely have to spend three nights on the road if it was in the same condition as when we came up. I surely wanted to beat any storm that may be brewing.

I don't talk much when I ride, but the trip back to Durango seemed like I was visiting the morgue. Molly was extremely quiet, almost to the point of pretending that I was not there. When I looked at her mother the during supper the second night, she just shrugged her shoulders. The road was better so it was a blessing that we only had to spend two nights on the trip. Mrs. Johnson checked the wounds every night and bound my ribs up tight. They weren't giving me any problems.

Kohlmeyer saw us arrive late in the evening and waved me over. He handed me a telegram which I opened on the wagon bench. I didn't realize that Molly was looking over my shoulder.

"Denver—STOP--arrive Jun 10."

It was signed, *Juanita*.

"Are you going?" she asked solemnly.

I didn't give a straight answer, probably because I didn't have one, but also I just wanted to be ornery and annoy her some, so I said, "Don't know, that's a few months away."

Her reply was a curt, "We'll get off here. Momma come on, let's go home."

It wasn't a long walk, and it was still light out though the sun had set. I almost chuckled when Molly slipped and if she hadn't been holding to her mother's arm would have fallen in the muddy street. She glanced back to see if I was laughing.

"I'll bring your suitcases around after I take the wagon to the livery," I said and snapped the reins. The mules were ready to get into the stall and eat. They took off with a jerk.

I was chuckling and shaking my head as I rode the few blocks to Kohlmeyer's livery. Women, no way to understand them. And in my life, recently, they have come in twos. Mother and daughter, woe is me. But instead of being depressed, I started hee-hawing like one of those old mules.

CHAPTER 19

Three days later I was on the road again, this time riding as a guard for wagons heading for Rico. There were eight wagons loaded with supplies for Telluride, but the pass was closed and they would be unloaded at Rico, stored there until the pass was open.

I had never been in this part of the country and was looking at more of the beauty of God's creation. My side was tender but I was able to ride Toit a full day. Molly had made me a bunch of fixin's for the first day and on top she placed a piece of pie.

There were eight teamsters and two others riding guard with me. There was no expectation of being robbed as we weren't carrying any money. It would be hard for a gang to take off with eight wagons.

It was nice during the day, but at night it was downright cold. The teamsters did all the work, all I and the other guards had to do was make the camp secure, check on the mules and stand guard during the night.

I lay in my soogan a spell. The sky was clear, that was one reason it was so cold. I didn't remember falling asleep. For some reason, the next morning as we went on our way I thought of that. Does anyone ever remember when they go to sleep? They can't remember that, but only the thoughts just prior to sleep taking them. Hmm, perhaps death is that way; it just sort of overtakes a person.

Like I said, I do quite a bit of pondering when I'm riding. The trail will do that to a person. It will make them a sure 'nuff philosopher of sorts or drive one to stark madness. Why I knew of cowboys that went plumb crazy living in line shack during the winter. Not all can handle that life, but then again we weren't meant to be hermits anyways.

That made me do more thinking along that line. Right off the start, the Bible says it is not good for man to be alone. Those thoughts were pestering me as Toit brought me around the bend of the grade we were climbing. I was the lead guard and I reined in Toit for a minute to look at the vast peaks of the Uncompahgres. My, my how majestic were those snow-covered peaks.

We were moving along the Dolores River and had just started to climb. The road narrowed leaving room for only one wagon. If wagons were to meet from different directions that could present a problem. There were cutoffs along the road, but to be in the right place didn't always happen.

At this time of year I didn't figure that there would be much traffic, but I wanted to be far enough out front so I could stop anyone traveling. Commerical wagons, such as ours, had to move during the winter whenever possible, but I didn't think there would be many others on the road.

I found out that I was wrong. I could see, just heading for the next bend a wagon with four people in it. Their wagon was loaded and it appeared to me that they might be moving. It didn't make much sense, moving in the middle of the winter.

Heading for them was a teamster with a loaded wagon. My mercy, the sky was turning blue with his oaths. He was sure blasting the man, and right in front of his missus and youngsters.

As I continued toward them, I saw the teamster take his whip, snapped it around the neck of the man jerking him off the wagon. The man fell hitting his head and was laying there in the mud and slush. I nudged Toit to move a little faster, but didn't want him to slip.

The teamster climbed down off his wagon heading for the family's wagon and began to push it. "Oh, Lord, help them," I cried aloud for he was trying to push them off the road. If they weren't killed they would still lose everything, probably their horses as well.

Still afraid to run Toit, I raised the Greener to fire then noticed how nervous the horses were. They were on the edge of the road and a shot might just scare them enough to get tangled and go over. The wagon was heavy and the man wasn't able to make much headway moving it. The woman was down out of the wagon grappling with the man trying to pull him away from the wagon. He gained control, slapped her, then shoved her to the ground. It was then I heard the little girl crying.

I couldn't wait, so I gave Toit a kick. We rushed toward them, and as I started to rein Toit in he slipped and slid right into the wagon. I went over him landing on the back of the wagon losing the grip on the shotgun. It fell where the woman was lying. Picking it up she swung it striking the teamster in the head, knocking him down and out.

Regaining my balance and composure I jumped down from the wagon. The husband was still out along with the teamster. I went to exam Toit who was bleeding from a cut; it looked as if he had twisted his front right leg. It didn't seem broken, but I noticed that he didn't put much weight on it. I looked at the woman, and I'm glad I did for her finger was on the trigger of the shotgun and it was pointed right at me.

Throwing my hands up I pleaded, "Ma'am, I'd appreciate it greatly if you'd remove your finger from that trigger. If it goes off more 'n' likely I'll be blasted to smitherin's and the horses will rear causing them to fall over the edge into the river taking the wagon and kids with them. Please, easy does it."

She came to her senses realizing what could transpire. I reached out and she handed me the shotgun. "We need to figure this out, and you need to check on your man."

I took the teamster's whip binding his arms together with it, and tied him to the wagon wheel. Looking up I gazed up the road then down to where our convoy was now stopped. I had to figure out a way so the wagons could pass. Walking up the road a piece I found where there was a little cut off. If I could get the teamster's wagon there, the others might just be able to pass.

Cal Clendenon, the driver of our first wagon watched as I began to unhitch the mules. He stepped down and began to help. Then we hitched them up to the back of the wagon.

He was scratching his chin, "I don't know Miles. Maybe..."

A couple of other men had now joined us. Cal was telling them the predicament and the plan. One went up with me to work with the mules, three others would take hold of the wagon tongue and try to guide the wagon.

The mules weren't used to pulling this way, so we had to coax them along. Finally, after some effort and the help of the other men in our group we moved the wagon up the road a piece where others could get by.

Picking up some snow from the shadows, I went back to where I tied the man to rub it in his face. He was semi-conscious, but this shocked him to full awareness.

"Mister, if you had just thought to be a little kinder and a little more careful your head wouldn't be sore and my horse wouldn't be hurt," I stated forcefully.

"The man you jerked off the wagon is still unconscious and we have loaded him into his wagon. You better hope he lives or your lack of restraint will make you a murderer. Now give me your name."

He was hesitant until he saw the boots of several men gather around. Teamsters stuck together, but they wouldn't put up with any shenanigans that would discredit their work.

"Cork O'Ryan," he replied. "I didn't mean no harm."

I was disgusted with his lack of remorse. "No matter, harm's done," I said, then got down in his face. "If he dies, I'll hunt you down."

Just for orneriness I took my knife and cut the whip that he was bound with. At least this ordeal would cost him something.

I knew I couldn't ride Toit and didn't know if the woman could handle the wagon with the slush and mud, so I climbed up into the seat and took the reins. I called Ben Martin over telling him that he was to take the lead and I would bring up the rear with this wagon.

"Ma'am, get yourself situated. I'll take you as far as Rico if'n that's the way you're goin'."

She turned to look at me with solemn features, then glanced back at her kids, the girl I had heard crying and a young lad. She nodded and we headed up the road following our little train. I stared at the man as I went past him.

CHAPTER 20

Just before arriving in Rico there was a cut-off to the East. The road was two ruts traveling out to some small farms. Ben said that he'd ride up with the wagons to the warehouse then come help me unload.

We rode perhaps half a mile when the woman pointed to a small house a little ways to the right of the road. Approaching it I could see that it was solidly built but rather small. Some work was needed on the barn and the corral was down in some places.

I reined up in front of the cabin. "You better stay here until I check it out," I stated getting down off the wagon with only a small twinge in my side.

Stepping on the porch I tried the door and found it unlocked. Pushing it open I stepped in. No one had been here in quite a spell, but it was quite musty and needed some cleaning.

Going back to the wagon I could see Ben riding up the road toward us. The woman was staring downward at the man bedded in the wagon bed.

"Do you think he'll be all right?" she asked.

Those were the first words she had said through the ordeal. I was thinking maybe she was dumb. "Not sure," I replied. "Head injuries like that are hard to figure. At least he is breathin' and hopefully he will regain consciousness."

"Why don't you go on in and get a place ready for us to lay him. Ben is almost here," I told her.

I helped her down off the wagon and she hurried in to fix up the bed. The two kids jumped off to follow her, the boy glancing up at me. Neither said anything. Quiet family, I thought to myself.

The woman was sweeping out the cabin when Ben dismounted tying his horse to the post on the front porch. "Help me carry him, Ben. She's got a bed ready for him."

When we came to the door she stepped inside before us, and we followed her to a room to the side. We laid him on the bed while she covered him with his coat.

She stood looking down at him for a minute or so, long enough that the silence became uncomfortable. Her hand went to her nose and mouth to cover a sniffle. The kids were at the foot of the bed watching. "Ma..." the boy started to speak when she held out her hand stopping him.

"Let's go out to the other room," she said.

I looked around. It was sparse. There was one table with two chairs in a bare kitchen. No stove, so she would be cooking over the fireplace or outside.

She grabbed the boy by the shoulder, "Go get some wood," she ordered. As he took off she hollered, "Don't forget some kindling."

Turning her attention to Ben and I, she began to apologize. "I'm sorry, my manners, I, uh, was sorta stunned by all that took place. My name is Catharine Innesberg, and this my husband George. Our children are Fredriech and Victoria. We were picking up the rest of our goods to move here as we are planning on starting a small farm. George has plans to raise horses.

I didn't say anything, but I wondered where the rest of their goods were. The town of Rico was situated along the Dolores River in a lush valley. There were several mines I spotted on the sides of the mountains especially to the north.

"Ma'am, we need to get a fire started," remarked Ben. "It's downright chilly, and it's going to get cold tonight. I hope you have plenty of wood cut."

She seemed to ignore him as she said to neither of us in particular. "I don't suppose there's a doctor in town."

We both shrugged our shoulders. "I don't know this settlement. We're just delivering supplies."

"Come on Ben, let's unload that wagon," I hinted starting for the door. "Ma'am, you can tell us where to place things."

Still no response. I didn't push her to talk for it seemed she was some apprehensive in doing so. It seemed actually that she was afraid to say something she shouldn't.

The boy came in with a couple of armloads of wood while we were unloading. I smiled as I saw the girl, maybe six or seven, carrying handfuls of sticks. It took about half and hour to unload. It was getting dark as the valley was surrounded by mountains.

"Ben, you better be gettin'," I said. "It's goin' to get cold. Tell Kohlmeyer to take me off the payroll until I get back. It might be a week, maybe two. I want to make sure things are all right here."

He nodded, "Sure will."

As he was riding off I headed to the door. "Ma'am, I goin' to put the mules and my horse in the barn. Be back in awhile."

I hadn't checked the barn yet; I hoped that there was room enough for their horses and Toit. To my pleasant surprise, there was plenty of hay and four stalls that had been cleaned. George must have cleaned up the barn before leaving.

After I unhitched the team I put them in the stalls with a bait of hay then rubbed them down. I wanted to check Toit's cut and leg before putting him in a stall.

"Sorry, old boy for neglecting you so long," I spoke to him, as I pulled off the saddle. There was water in the trough by the corral, so I let him drink while I wiped off the cut. Not deep, I'd clean it up good in the light tomorrow. He limped slightly as he walked. I wouldn't be able to ride him for at least a week.

After rubbing him down and putting him in a stall with plenty of hay, I took the two horses out to drink. It had been quite a day for man and for beast.

Back in the barn I looked around. I had to shake my head, thoughts of two years ago came to my mind when I spent the winter in the barn. There was a lantern hanging from a hook. I checked it for oil finding it was near full, so I went ahead and lit it so I could see when I came back for the night.

When I came back to the house I was greeted by a warm fire blazing in the fireplace and the aroma of coffee. Mrs. Innesberg was stooped down frying up bacon in a skillet. The two children were sitting on the chairs by the table. They were sure quiet.

Pouring me some coffee, she looked at me, "I'm sorry, tomorrow I'll make a better breakfast." Then turning her attention to the children. "Victoria, get the plates for the bacon.

In a few minutes, she and I were at the table eating while the kids sat on the floor near the fireplace. I looked to see if there was wood enough to see them through the night.

She watched me look around the room. "As soon as George is better, he plans on adding an additional room for the children," she informed me then dropped her head.

It alarmed me some, "Are you all right?" I asked earnestly as she began to softly sob.

"Yes, yes, I'm fine. I have never thanked you for what you did and are doing. I'm ashamed of that."

"Ahh, don't let that bother you. You've had plenty on your mind. With the accident, the fight, your husband laid up, and taking care of two kids, it's a wonder you've made supper," I chuckled a little.

"I don't even know your name," she lamented. "I should at least know who helped us."

I smiled, "Miles Forrest, Ma'am. Glad to meet you."

She attempted to return the smile. She just couldn't quite get it done. Maybe tomorrow after a night's rest.

Getting up I went to the fire to pour another cup. "Mind if I take this with me? I need to get my bedding fixed."

That got her attention. "Oh, you can't, you mustn't sleep in the barn. It's too cold."

I looked around the room. "Yes Ma'am, I'll be quite all right." I didn't tell her that I'd spent a winter in a barn and near froze to death.

CHAPTER 21

I had been up for a while but didn't want to bother those in the house. I checked on Toit and then looked through the barn for some kind of ointment. Finding none, I took him out for a drink and with my bandanna washed the cut. It didn't look bad; maybe I worry too much, but he was a good friend.

While out there I surveyed the barn, corral, and house. I noticed that there was about half a cord of wood cut. That wouldn't come close to getting them through the winter.

Taking Toit back to the barn I watched carefully to see if he was still limping. Not as noticeably as yesterday, but he was still favoring it some. It would be best to rest him for a week.

"Mister Forrest! Come quick!" came a yell from the house. I had just tossed Toit some fresh hay. I rushed to the house then noticed that I still had the hay rake in my hand. I placed it against the wall then went on in.

The two children were still in their nightclothes standing in the doorway to the bedroom. "No, George, you mustn't get up," I heard Mrs. Innesberg's exasperated voice.

Pushing through the children I saw her trying to hold her husband down. He was fighting against her so I pushed on his shoulders. His wild eyes looked at me then threw a punch. There was no power or direction in it. He was conscious but completely confused of his surroundings.

He seemed to settle down so I released him and glanced at the children who had been watching the spectacle. Mrs. Innesberg gave a heavy sigh and moved away from the bed to check on the children.

As soon as she left he threw his legs over the side of the bed to stand. "No, George!" she screamed.

Some men are just hardheaded enough to try something when they know they shouldn't, just ask me and I'll tell you. He stood, weaving, then made a half turn and began to churn his head round and round. Both Mrs. Innesberg and I hurried to him catching him just before he fell.

We finally got him settled back in the bed. "Get a wet cloth," I commanded. The boy Fredriech ran to the bucket and shortly he was back with the cloth.

"Who are you?" he mumbled as his wife laid the cool cloth on his head.

"Never mind right now," I replied. "Can you remember anything that happened?"

He was slow in talking but seemed to get most of it right. His eyes moved back in forth, nervous like, but I reckoned a knock on the head could do that to a person. "Catharine," he said reaching out his hand. "Are you, are the children all right?"

She sat on the edge of the bed holding his hand and patting him on the chest. "Yes, George, we're all fine."

His cheeks moved upward as to try to smile and I could see his eyes stop fidgeting then he closed them. I think this time he was sleeping.

"Stay by his side," I said, then looked at the children. "You eaten?"

They both shook their heads. "Well show me the fixin's and I'll get something started."

Victoria took me by my finger to pull me toward the counter in the kitchen. Then smiling she pointed. There was flour, saleratus, lard, salt, and some cans of condensed milk. I rolled up my sleeves and began to work.

Before long I had a dozen biscuits ready, just needed to prepare the Dutch oven. I'd let them cook some, then fry up some bacon.

"Coffee's already on," said Fredriech solemnly. After I set the Dutch oven in the coals I took the pot and poured me a cup.

It wasn't long before Mrs. Innesberg came from the bedroom. I had noticed that she was a slight woman the other day, but seeing her come through that doorway she looked downright skinny. There didn't look to be any meat on her bones.

She was holding to the back of a chair. "Go ahead and sit, Ma'am. Victoria, do you think you could carry a cup of coffee to your mother? Careful now, don't spill any of it on you as it's hot."

I filled the cup half full and she walked gingerly toward her mother. She smiled when the cup was handed to her.

Taking a sip, she looked at me. "I heard him retching some time this morning. I went to check on him and he was sleeping. At least he is alive."

"Ma'am, it might be a day or two, but he'll pull out of it. Why if nothin' else to see his wife and younguns. We'll have some breakfast and then maybe Fred could show..."

"Fredriech," she said emotionless.

"Fredriech could show me where I could find some wood to haul to the house. You've not near enough for the winter."

She didn't answer. I looked at the boy and he was staring at his mother. Finally she replied, "I suppose so."

We ate all the biscuits and bacon that I'd fried. I asked if she kept a can for the bacon grease and she pointed to the counter. I poured most of it in the can, but kept a dab out so I could sop it with my last biscuit.

"I'll go hitch up the team while you get the boy ready," I said then stood to head to the barn.

Fredriech and I made a dozen trips hauling in branches and small timber. I had to cut some of it up in the woods before we could load it in the wagon. The boy was small, but he worked. I let him help me with the larger logs, but it was more for his good than the help he gave me.

After lunch I'd start the chopping. I'd put him to work cutting up kindling and stocking the woodpile. It was winter, and a storm could come at any time. I had to get some of this done.

The mountains were white, and there was snow in the shadows where the sun couldn't hit it. The temperature was probably in the forties, and dropped to the teens at night. The sky was still clear but that could change at a moment's notice, especially here in the high country.

CHAPTER 22

For the next several days I worked at the woodpile then went to mending the corral. Fredriech helped the best he could. I tried to get him to talking, but for the most part kept silent.

Mister Innesberg was conscious but had to be helped wherever he wanted to go. Whenever attempting to stand he said the room would begin to whirl. I hoped he would be getting better soon or I'd lose my job at Kohlmeyer's.

It was on the third day that Mrs. Innesberg gave me some money to buy supplies from town. She was working inside the house, trying to square things away putting them where she wanted.

I went to Callahan's general merchandise to get the goods on the list. "So you must be the Good Samaritan that is helping at the Innesberg's. Glad to meet you," he said offering his hand then taking the note that I was holding in the other hand. "I'll get Nathan to get this together and load it in your wagon."

He left, going to the backroom and returning with a tall, lanky young man who immediately began filling the order. Then coming back to me, he motioned toward a couple of chairs by the stove that had a checkerboard between them.

"What was it that happened? I heard that George could quite a knock to the ol' noggin'."

I filled him in on what had taken place. He would grunt, or hum. Once in a while he would say, "my, my," but mostly listened.

"I must say," he stated when I finished, "that you're quite a man to be helping out. I don't know much about them. George came in about two months ago, purchased the little ranch, fixed it up some, then told me he was going after his wife and kids and would be gone a few weeks."

He paused when Nathan came in notifying us that the wagon was loaded and asking if there was anything he could do for me. I shook my head starting to get up when Mr. Callahan started talking again.

"Rico, we're a nice, rich, hidden secret. Most of the talk is about Telluride, but the mines around here are producing, producing plenty. We've a fine hotel, two restaurants and the Bon Ton can't be beat for food. Best this side of the divide until you get to San Francisco. Of course, we've got our share of saloons, none of them fit to visit except perhaps Lovejoy's."

He looked at me, then sort of got embarrassed. "Sorry, I was running off at the mouth. Like I said, I don't know much about George so you be sure you take care out there." He reached out his hand as I departed. "Name's Barney."

When I arrived back at the house, Mrs. Innesberg and Fredriech must have seen me coming for they were waiting to help me unload. With their help it didn't take long. I handed her the money that was left over then took the wagon on to the barn.

Unhitching the horses, I took them to the trough talking to them while they drank. "Bought you hard workers a treat. You'll find out when I put you in the stall."

I had purchased several bags of oats. It's good to have some for the horses. I get tired of eating the same old thing so I reckon the horses get tired of eating hay all the time.

Toit told me that he appreciated it, at least that what I took him to say when he shook his head as I gave him some feed. I had just finished rubbing down the horses and feeding them when Victoria came to let me know that lunch was ready.

It wasn't a big affair, but it was a change. Mrs. Innesberg had cut up some of one of the hams I purchased, and while I was gone had made bread. She made a tasty ham sandwich and had some special kind of mustard on it. I hadn't tasted mustard like that since I left the Hill Country of Texas.

George seemed some better as he was able to sit up at the table without weaving. He gave a grim smile at his wife then informed me, "I can walk from the bedroom to the table on my own."

I didn't say anything just chewed on my sandwich and drank my coffee. That was improvement, maybe by next week I could make my way back to Durango.

After lunch I was back out working on the wood. Looking up I saw three riders coming up the road. I drove the axe into a stump, put on my gunbelt, and picked up the Greener watching them approach. They were not drifters and had the look of wannabe hard-cases. They stopped a short distance from me, looking around at the place.

The rider in the middle, who was a thick-looking man, and by that I don't mean fat spoke up. "We're looking for the Innesberg place."

All three of the men wore jackets, but I could see they were open with their guns visible. "My name is Forrest," I replied.

Anger appeared on the man's face and his forehead looked like an accordion with all the wrinkles. "I don't care what your name is, tell me if this is the Innesberg place!" he snapped.

The man on the left looked familiar to me, then I remembered and smiled. My attention went back to the man who had spoken. "Right now, Mr. Innesberg is indisposed, you can speak to me."

He didn't like my answer for a slight sneer appeared on his face. I looked at the man I recognized. "You doin' Hanks' dirty work now?"

Squinting he searched my face. "Mister Forrest, Innesberg has something that belongs to the Bishop in Moab. We're here to fetch it for him."

I brought the shotgun up cocking it. "Tell that man on the right if he moves his hand another inch toward his gun the lot of you will face a load of double-ought shot."

The man I spoke about was a small, gaunt-looking man. He was near paper thin, and his eyes were close together sunk deep into his head. There was something evil in his appearance.

"You tell Hanks, personally from me, to leave the Innesbergs alone. If not, I'll come for him personally. Savvy?"

I had met Jacob Hanks a few years back. He was riding with Porter Rockwell and Lot Smith enforcing the dictates of the Prophet in Salt Lake City. Rockwell was dead now and Smith had moved to southern Utah to hunt wild horses.

"We can't leave without them," he replied.

I shook my head. "What's your name?" I asked.

He hesitated looking at the lead rider. "Shame," I breathed. "Always like to know the names of the men I kill. Plus when I meet with Hanks over this I can tell him why his people died."

The big man spoke. I'm Tim Collins, that fellow you're jawin' with is Amos Yarnell." He stopped, not giving the name of the scrawny man.

I took a couple steps to my right to confront the thin man. "And you. Do you have a name?"

He blasted forth with an oath. I raised the Greener. "My, my, what would the Bishop say to that filthy mouth?"

I could tell he was itching to go for his gun, but a shotgun looking in your face had a tendency to make you think twice. "Your name?"

"Loyal Reems," he spat out.

"Mr. Collins, Yarnell, why don't you back away. Go back to Hanks, tell him you couldn't find Innesberg, or tell him I sent you packing," I stressed, keeping the shotgun on Reems.

Collins wiped his mouth with his hand a couple of times and without saying anything turned his horse back toward town. I didn't lower the shotgun, but I nodded at Yarnell who returned with one of his own.

The two men were riding back toward Rico, Reems was sitting facing me. "Your choice," I stated.

He pulled his hat down tight, then kicked his horse racing to catch up with the others. Lowering the shotgun, I thought that if Lot Smith was here that fellow would be hearing from him about the way he treats his horse.

I turned to go to the house where I saw Mrs. Innesberg in the doorway. There's some explaining to be done.

CHAPTER 23

She stood in the doorway, the back of her fist to her mouth in fear. As I entered, George was at the table his head down, held between his hands. I went directly to the table with Mrs. Innesberg following me.

"All right," I started with a firm voice. "Tell me what is goin' on here. Those three Mormon hunters weren't here for pleasure."

Innesberg after all of his ordeal had looked better then than he did now, with his face drawn and pale. The corners of his eyes were etched in fear and his eyes fluttered from me to his wife.

Turning to his wife, I asked sternly, "If he won't say, maybe you have the gumption to talk." I was becoming a mite agitated.

"She's not my wife!" he yelled startling me. "She's not my wife," he began to moan, "she's my sister. When her husband died, the Bishop took her for one of his wives. I wasn't about to let my sister be a Mormon wife and have her kids raised that way. I went and got her," he said ending with a deep sigh.

My attention returned to him, "Well, you got a heap of trouble. They won't give up easily. But you better make things right with the folks around here. Let them know the truth. Neighbors can be mighty helpful when they know you are straight with them."

Pulling on the edge of my moustache, twisting it I thought for a minute. "I'd start with Mr. Callahan in Rico. Tell him and the others what happened."

He was frowning as was, well, Catharine now that I knew she wasn't Mrs. Innesberg. "I don't think I can face them," he murmured.

"Well, you better!" I exclaimed. "They'll understand more than you think."

Catharine, Mrs. Innesberg, or whoever she was stayed pretty much away from me the rest of the day. I'd stay on a few more days, to help out until I was sure that Innesberg could do regular chores and to make sure they weren't bothered no more by Collins.

It was quiet that night at supper. The kids had their meals and were sitting on the floor by the fireplace. I was on a barrel at the table with the Innesbergs. They seemed both to be depressed, more him than her.

"Don't judge us too severely, Mr. Forrest. George was only trying to protect me and the children," she said softly as she passed the plate of biscuits.

"Ma'am, Mrs., uh. I'm not judgin' you at all. I can understand the situation, but it's not good to be hidin' it," I said removing a couple of biscuits to go with the fried ham and onions.

"George," I called him out on purpose. "You have to man-up. Get this house and your spread to doin' something. Don't be moping around, frettin.'"

He lifted his eyes briefly to look at me. "Listen, I reckon those fellows are stayin' in Rico. I'll go down after supper and have another talk with them. I don't think that you'll have trouble with Collins and Yarnell, but that other man is a varmint."

I took a bite of biscuit and started chewing, all the while my attention darting back and forth from the two people. It was Catharine that began to speak. "My name is Catharine Myers. My husband, Clinton and I had a little place near Grand Junction. When Clinton died, I caught the attention of Bishop Malone. He and some men were in the town on business."

She stopped, catching her breath before continuing. "A few weeks later a group of men came and took me and the kids with them to Utah. I had been in correspondence with George and soon he came to town."

"I found out through friends what had happened," George took up the conversation. "I didn't know where they went, just to Utah. I went to town and began questioning folks there. I was informed that the Bishop and some men were in town earlier that month, and found out the Bishop's name was Malone and that he lived in Moab."

I listened intently to their story. "How were you able to get her back?" I asked.

He smiled for the first time that I had known him. "I made sure that she saw me after I found out that she was there. She was kept off to a room at the back corner of the house. I went there one night and we were able to talk. We made plans to leave in two nights so she could make sure the kids were with her in the room."

Leaning back, I forgot I was sitting on a barrel and almost fell off. Laughing, I told him, "Go on, that doesn't tell me how you got them out."

"Diversion," he said quietly. "There were bars on that window so she couldn't sneak out that way so I created a diversion... I set fire to the barn at the edge of town. Then while everyone was out looking at the fire, she grabbed the kids and came to where I had horses."

"We rode hard back to her place in Grand Junction where I traded the horses for draft ones and took the wagon from Clinton's place and we headed here."

I sat there, pulling on the other side of my moustache, then I rubbed my hand down over my mouth and chin. "Let's all go to town. There's a little light left and I have a nickel for each of the kids. You four can go to Callahan's and properly introduce yourselves and I'll have a talk with those Mormons."

Twenty minutes later we were on the road. It was twilight and would be dark by the time we arrived in town. I left them with the wagon at the store and walked down to where I saw the horses tied to a post. It just happened to be in front of one of the saloons in town. Nice place for God-fearing folk, I though to myself.

Standing just outside the door, I peered inside before entering. I'd entered too many saloons in my duties as a Ranger to go barging in without checking the place out first. The ones I was looking for were sitting at a table in the far corner. Three others were in the saloon, one at the bar, the other two at a front table.

"Howdy boys," I hollered, giving them a big smile. Two of them were drinking whiskey, Yarnell was just sitting there. "Didn't mean to catch you in your vice. Why the ol' Patriarch in Salt Lake would sure like to see how his Zionists act away from home."

Yarnell nodded at me. Reems, was sitting closest to me, stood to his feet and went for his gun. Mine was out first before his even cleared leather and up against his breadbasket. I said quietly, "Be sure you're ready for the Judgment, and from the looks of things you might want to consider carefully your next action."

He proceeded to pronounce an epithet that wouldn't be fitting to repeat anywhere. I looked at Yarnell, then hit the man in the mouth with my gun. He dropped instantly to the floor.

I hadn't bothered to look at Collins save a glance when I came to the table. He may be in charge, but I had an acquaintance with Yarnell. "Mind if I sit?" I didn't wait for an answer but moved the chair away from the one on the floor and sat down.

"Do you know the story?"

"Don't matter," said Collins. "We were told to bring her back."

The Greener was in my left hand and I placed it on the table, just for effect. Yarnell looked at me, but I could see Collins' attention going to the shotgun.

"Yarnell, you know me. I mean what I say. If I hear of anything I will go to Hanks first and then I'll find you and your friends."

I smiled, my focus now going to Collins. "Or if'n you have a notion, we can take care of this now and you won't have to worry about seein' Hanks."

Collins was a little concerned, but Yarnell had already made up his mind what he was going to do. "Forrest, I heard Lot Smith talk about you. I remember you and what you did for those two women that winter. You're a hard man, but fair. We'll be going."

"Might as well stay the night and leave in the morning, but I'd go before you get snowed in," I told them.

I stood up, holstered my pistol turning to walk out when Yarnell spoke up. "Forrest, I can't speak for Reems. I'd watch my back."

"Amos," I replied using his Christian name, "I'd be more careful of the company I keep." I touched the brim of my hat with the Greener then left.

CHAPTER 24

I was up early the next morning, saddled Toit and went to town. It was my plan to eat some breakfast at the Bon Ton watching for my "friends" to eat then leave town.

The food was good, the biscuits light, and the coffee strong. A person can't ask for much more than that. I was just finishing up when the three walked through the door. Collins immediately saw me, then elbowed Yarnell who nodded. Reems didn't bother to glance my way, in fact, he walked with his head down.

Since I was finished I paid, what I thought was a steep amount, six-bits, but then again this was a mining town, and went outside. The sun was coming up behind one of the peaks, and I found a seat where it could warm me as there was a chill in the air. I reckoned the weather would be changing soon.

Thirty minutes later the three men came out and mounted. Yarnell gave a slight wave, then they kicked their horses into a gallop out of town. I sat there a moment longer watching them while rubbing the whiskers on my chin. I didn't think they would bother the Innesbergs anymore. Folks just don't take to wife or sister stealing, especially if there are children involved.

When I got back to the house George Innesberg was coming from the barn. Dismounting I tied Toit by the water trough then approached Innesberg.

"I watched the men leave," I told him. "I don't think they'll bother you again."

I was glad to see that he was able to walk and was up doing some chores. He had been in the barn feeding the horses. "Catharine has breakfast ready, come on in," he said.

My stomach was satisfied, but thought I should go in to be hospitable and enjoy the company. Plus I could always drink another cup of coffee.

The atmosphere had changed in the cabin. It was lighter, less stress. Catharine was even humming some tune as she filled my cup.

"Good to see you're up and around," I noted speaking to George. "How's your head?"

His hand went to touch where he had been hit. "Little sore, but the dizziness is gone. I'll be all right now."

He began to spoon down some kind of porridge, I reckoned was oatmeal. I don't mind the stuff, but I'd rather have eggs along with biscuits and gravy. But each has his own taste.

Catharine cleared her throat with a cough, took a sip of coffee then addressed me. "Mr. Forrest, we are truly beholding to you. We'll never be able to repay you."

"Already have," I said smiling. "New friends, that's payment enough." I paused to take a sip. "Figure I'll finished chopping the wood and if you're able to help, get that corral finished before I leave."

"Leave?" questioned Catharine. "Do you think George is ready to work?"

He nodded, "Ready, fit, and able. Tell me what needs to be done?"

"I'll work on that wood while you and Fred," I stopped to look at Catharine to see if she would correct me—she didn't. "While you and Fred haul down some more. When the snow settles in for the winter, you'll want to have more than enough to get you through. When you get back we'll finish the corral, that shouldn't take too long."

I stayed three more days with George and Catharine. He planned on building a small cabin with two rooms for Catharine and the kids. He also told me his plans for raising horses. He was planning on raising Morgans. I told him about Pennington over Gunnison way raising his own alfalfa.

When I rode out, the sun was no longer shining and it was threatening to snow. I was leaving at a good time. I told them that I'd ride through now and then to check on how they were doing.

By the time I reached Big Bend, the snow was falling regular. It wasn't hard, but steady and just beginning to build up. The hostler said that he had a couple of beds where he stayed and I could spend the night there. From there, if there wasn't too much snow I could make it to Durango the next day.

Kohlmeyer was glad to see me when I arrived for work the next day. He didn't pay me while I was gone, but he kept my spot open.

Benj was with him in his office sharing coffee and lies along with a couple of teamsters. "Yuh seen that gal yet?" he asked me.

"What gal?" I replied honestly.

"Don't give me that," he guffawed along with the other men.

"Forrest," began one of the other men, "If you don't shake a leg and tell her yur feelings, well, then I reckon I'll start courtin' her."

Kohlmeyer had been laughing with the others then he put his big paw on my shoulder. "She's asked about you near every day." Then he turned me, giving me a little shove toward the door.

That brought a mite of laughter from the men. I didn't give them the satisfaction of looking back at them, but went on out into the falling snow. It was still falling steadily, but only about six inches accumulation.

I didn't really want to go up to Molly's house and invite myself in, but that seemed to be my only choice. The fire had put them out of business and I didn't know if they had found another place yet.

Knocking on the door, it was opened by Mrs. Johnson. "Why Miles, welcome back. Come on in. Molly! You have a visitor. Here, let me have your coat. Go on in by the fire."

First thing I did was take my hat off, then fumbled with my coat since I had my hat in my hand. But soon everything was fine and I was standing by the fire. The warmth felt good especially after a couple of days riding in the snow.

I looked at the flames, then my gaze moved up to the mantle and on around the room. It was sparsely decorated with only a couple of chairs in the room. About half-way in my survey I saw Molly standing in the little hall between the main room and the dining room. She had her hands on her hips, and a solemn look on her face.

What did I expect? I didn't figure she would come running to my arms. Or was that a subconscious thing in my thick head?

She took a couple of steps into the room. "Hungry?" she asked.

I smiled turning toward her. "Mother is making breakfast, you'll be joining us."

It was a matter-of-fact statement, no asking about it. What else could I reply, but "I'd love to."

"We didn't know you were back in town or she would have had biscuits in the oven. Silas Horner, I don't think you know him, brought us a load of elk meat a couple of days ago. Momma is frying up some chops."

Molly motioned to one of the chairs. I sort of stumbled toward it as I wanted to keep looking at her. This morning she had her hair up and was wearing a tan corduroy skirt and a yellow and black checkered flannel shirt. Nor real fancy, or fashionable, but it fit her.

She went to the other chair and we scooted them closer to the fire. I told her of the ordeal that took place with the Innesbergs and why I stayed longer.

"I heard from Mr. Kohlmeyer. Ben Martin told him of the incident on the road," she paused, looking down at her hands, then over to me. "Seems you're a regular good Samaritan."

I wondered how she meant that. It almost seemed like she thought I shouldn't have gotten involved. I told her about the kids, and finding out that she wasn't George's wife. Maybe I shouldn't have, but I also told her of the fight with the Mormons.

"It's time!" came the voice from the other room.

Not that I minded talking with Molly, but the time was well spent with her mother making cornbread to go along with the chops, eggs, and gravy. Not your regular breakfast, but then I wondered, what is?

We sat down and bowed our heads as Mrs. Johnson said a simple blessing over the food. As we were filling our plates, she turned to Molly. "Did you give him the telegrams?"

Molly shook her head, then said, "I'll get them. I was going to let Miles eat first."

My eyes went to Molly then over to her mother all the time I was chewing a tender piece of elk. Molly got up going over to a small desk in the corner to pick up two telegrams, then brought them to me.

I glanced at them while I continued eating. One was from Dave Cook, the other from Juanita. Hmm...I thought it best to finish my breakfast.

Molly and her mother folded their hands in front of them while I continued to eat. I looked at her, once smiling, then went back to my food.

Mrs. Johnson brought her hands to her mouth to suppress a smile or maybe even a little giggle. Molly had unfolded her hands by this time and was tapping on the table with one, getting a scolding look from her mother.

"Fine breakfast," I announced patting my stomach. Giving Mrs. Johnson a smile, "Thank you very much."

She knew I was being ornery and giggled out loud this time. Now it was Molly's turn to glare at her which almost brought a laugh from me.

I thought about getting up and not reading the telegrams until I was back in my room, but then I might be on the receiving end of a plate thrown at me.

Reaching for Cook's, I read:

Job available—STOP--Elias in Central City
"Hmmm," I sighed.

Reaching for the one from Juanita I fumbled with it, then half-dropped it before finally getting it opened. I read this one to myself. Then looked up at the ladies with a smile on my face.

In Denver, June 10—STOP--Hope to see you.

I folded both notes and placed them inside my vest.

"Are you going?" came the whispered voice from Molly.

Pulling on the end of my moustache I replied, "I don't know. I already have a job." Then I looked directly at Molly, "What do you think I should do?"

She wasn't expecting that, and blushed. Trying to stammer out an answer she said, "That's up to you." Then she stood and began clearing the dishes off the table.

CHAPTER 25

The snow was still falling when I left Molly and didn't look like it was going to let up anytime soon. I was on my way to visit Toit when Ben Martin hollered at me. "Mr. Kohlmeyer wants to meet with us all at the warehouse!"

It was a few blocks over and with the snow the ground was now solid, not slush or puddles. Upon entering the front area of the warehouse I saw several teamsters and guards all talking and chattering to each other. The room was warm and felt nice after coming in from the cold.

I moved over to a corner and leaned against the wall to wait. It was fifteen, maybe twenty minutes before all of us were there, then Mr. Kohlmeyer came from his office along with another man who stayed by the office door.

His countenance was downcast with a glum, grim look. The men gave way as he strode to the center of the crowd. "Men, now understand, this doesn't give me pleasure, but I'm going to have to let several of you go. It's nothing personal nor a reflection on your job," he stopped to clear his voice. "The reality is that the passes are closed, winter has set in and I've very little work."

That brought a low murmur from the men gathered. Months without pay, and very few in town were hiring that I knew of. I looked at some of the men I knew. Some were married with a family, it was going to be tough on them.

Kohlmeyer must have sensed what I was thinking. "Men, don't hesitate to see me if you need food for your family. I won't see anyone starved."

He looked at the crowd. "Fresno, Cork, Benj," he called out. Men were watching, listening anxiously for their name. He called out a couple more then finished, "Sorry men, that's all; come see me after lunch for your final pay."

I had to shake my head. What was I just telling Molly—I had a job. Now, just like that, it was gone. Life sure has a way of playing the joker at times.

The men, disgruntled but understanding started to leave the warehouse. I imagine some wondering why the ones chosen were and they were not, but not bitter at Kohlmeyer. They understood that was the breaks in life.

I started to move out with them when I heard, "Forrest, hold on!"

Stopping I looked toward Mr. Kohlmeyer who was motioning for me to come his way. When I approached I saw the stranger standing alongside Mr. Kohlmeyer.

"Miles, this is Jim Hill, he works for Wells Fargo," he said upon introduction.

I reached out my hand, "Glad to meet you." He had a firm grip and we looked each other in the eyes. There is something about shaking a man's hand and looking in their eyes to get a viable first impression.

"Mr. Forrest. I'll come right to the matter at hand. The messenger on the stage from here to Cortez broke his leg and won't be able to work for several weeks. I need a man riding shotgun in his place."

He stopped to gaze at my expression. "Mind you, it's only part time, until he recovers, but it will put some change in your pockets."

"I'm interested," I told him immediately. He then began to tell me particulars. "Monday the stage leaves for Cortez, where you will stay overnight, then return to Durango on Tuesday. On Thursday, you will head to Cortez again, returning on Friday.

"Come down to the office this afternoon and I'll go over the company policies and procedures," he said reaching out his hand again. Then took Kohlmeyers, "Thanks, Vern."

I stood there as he left then glanced at Mr. Kohlmeyer who nodded his head then spoke to me. "Come spring, I'll need you to head to Alamosa to herd some stock back here for me, so don't get too attached."

Pulling on my moustache I hesitated to ask, but finally blurted, "Can I keep my little room? I'll pay what I can."

He chuckled. "Keep it, no charge."

I went back to my little room. It was chilled, the coals in the stove nearly cold. I stirred up the coals, put in some kindling to get it ablaze. Before long it was warm enough for me to take off my coat.

Sitting down on the cot I began to ponder what had transpired that day. I was sorely tempted to take Cook's job, but really didn't want to leave Durango, or was it Molly? That was something weighing on my mind. I wasn't hankering to see Juanita. She was a place in my past, something that might have been, but in the Lord's providence, wasn't to be.

The messenger for Wells Fargo wasn't a hard job and it was money for the time being. I decided to write Cook a letter explaining, and would send a short telegram to Juanita. No explanation was needed to her.

I laid back on my cot, enjoying the warmth of the room and began to pray. It must have been an hour later that I woke. The fire was down in the stove and instead of building it up again, I decided to go let Molly know what I decided to do then head on down to Wells Fargo.

CHAPTER 26

It was six weeks before Tom Larson was able to come back to his position. It was an easy job, sitting on top of the stage and sometimes holding on for dear life depending on who was doing the driving that day.

I worked Monday and Tuesday, Thursday and Friday. Easy money, but boring. The first couple of trips were exciting as I was traveling through new country for me, but after that it was the same trip.

And cold, my mercy! The stage may be late sometimes, but it never stopped. Higgins, one of the drivers, taught me a trick. At every stage stop he had stones being warmed in the stove. He'd wrap them in blankets and put them around his feet. Of course, before too long the rocks would cool off, but it was nice comfort for a while.

During that time I helped Molly and Mrs. Johnson locate a new place for their eatery. They ordered some bowls and plates along with some silverware. Mr. Kohlmeyer rounded up a few of the boys to help move the stove from the old place. The fire didn't hurt it none, just blackened it some.

They were good men, willing to help. They went from store to store looking for tables and chairs. Before the middle of January, the Johnson eatery was up and running. They didn't have much on the menu: stews, soups, and chili, but it was welcome and Mrs. Johnson was smiling again. Work is something that helps a person's soul.

The old pot-bellied stove that sat in front of the old eatery was now to the back near the counter. The kitchen was much larger and when Doc Shores sent the new stove there was plenty of room for it. The kitchen even had an inside pump; that in itself was a Godsend.

Kohlmeyer was not hiring yet as the passes to Telluride and Silverton were still closed. He kept the few men working around town, and made a few trips to Pagosa Springs and over to Cortez. Since I was now unemployed again, I spent time cutting wood for Mrs. Johnson and some of the other businesses in town. I made a dime here and there, enough to keep me in pie at the eatery.

Spring was coming, at least in Durango. Oh, it still snowed, but the days were warmer and the snow would quickly melt. Mr. Kohlmeyer came to me one sunny day.

"I'm told that you can make it over Wolf Creek now. Wagons still can't but a rider can. If you want the job I have some mules and horses waiting for me in Alamosa."

I was glad to have it. It would take about six days to get there and maybe ten coming back. He would pay me sixty dollars for the trip and pay for any supplies or incidentals I might need.

Molly was somewhat concerned about my making the trip with so much snow still in the high country, and there was always that chance a major storm could arise. I didn't want her fretting none, but it sort of made my heart warm that she had some feelings for me.

The trip over wasn't bad at all. The major problem was finding a dry place to throw my bedroll at night, but other than that the trip was smooth. Toit seemed to stumble once in a while and that concerned me. It just wasn't like him, but I couldn't find anything wrong with his legs.

When I arrived in Alamosa I was to look up a Norman Jessup, whom I found in the Gilded Cage. He was drinking and playing cards, politely excusing himself when I introduced myself. I was informed that his wrangler would be bring the horses in tomorrow, a dozen Percherons. I also had another dozen mules waiting for me.

After putting Toit up at the livery I got my room and threw my gear in it. I had to smile when I looked at the bed; it sure would be nice after some cold nights on the trail. Each room had a small fireplace with some wood by it, enough to keep the chill off.

I went down to the lobby asking about a place to eat and was informed that the place next door was the best in town. Thanking the clerk, I walked toward the restaurant thinking, yeah, I wonder how much he receives for saying that.

The place was relatively busy and that was a good sign. I started to take a table by the window when I thought I recognized someone so I decided to go to his table.

"Father Dyer, how in the world are you?" I asked whole-heartedly.

He looked up holding a piece of steak on his fork squinting at me. "Son, I'm sorry."

I interrupted, "Mind if I join you. I don't expect you to remember me. It's been a while, five years or so over in Gunnison."

Reaching out my hand, he lowered the fork to shake it. "Miles Forrest, I was working for Pennington and met you."

"Henrietta! Yes, yes, you were the foreman. How are you?" he said, his eyes lighting up.

While we were chatting, I watched the waitress, a tiny, little gal. Wondering how she could carry that big coffeepot around to fill up cups. She looked so frail. The place was filling up when I received my order of pork chops, potatoes, and cabbage.

I had just taken a bite of the potatoes when some hardcases came to the table. "You two have to move, that's our table!" bellowed one of the men.

Wiping my mouth with the back of my hand I started to stand when the preacher motioned for me to stay seated. He stood up facing them, and the words from his mouth came so smoothly and genuinely.

"Boys," he said looking at the one who had spoken. "You have three options: you can fight over something stupid like a table and chairs with someone getting hurt over a piece of wood, or you can grab a chair and join us. We'll make room and won't mind the company, or you can sit at that table over there. What will it be?"

The three men looked at him. The spokesman smiled and tipped his hat. "Sorry, preacher-man, we'll just sit over yonder."

As they moved away, Father Dyer looked at me. "See Miles, not everything has to be handled with a gun or fists."

I nodded my head in agreement, then asked, "What would you have done if he had chosen the first option?"

That brought a large grin, he winked saying, "I figured you could handle the three of them."

We both dug into our food. I will have to apologize for my thoughts about the hotel clerk, this food was good.

"Miles, you did save room for some pie?" he inquired.

I smiled, "Always."

We both had a piece of butterscotch pie and then he became silent. I watched him close his eyes after he laid his fork on the plate. His lips were moving slightly. After a few minutes, he picked up the fork to finish the pie.

I was drinking my coffee when he asked, "Miles, have you ever seen the 'Devil's Grin'?"

My eyes widened and I lowered my cup. Looking him in the face, I sighed. "Parson, many times, too many times."

"Death seeks you," he told me solemnly. "I am to tell you to be strong and stay alert," then he smiled giving me some comfort. "Death will not take you for a while."

We were full. It had been a satisfying supper and the company was also satisfying, even with his warning to me.

"I'll be heading for Fairplay in the morning. I don't usually make it this far south, now I know," he said with a smile, "the reason for the visit."

He placed his hand on my shoulder and prayed then went on out the door. I had to laugh, gaining the attention of the nearby tables. He left me with the bill, but I'd plan on paying for his meal anyway.

CHAPTER 27

The horses arrived mid-morning. I went to the corral to look them over. *Twenty-four horses and mules,* I began to think shaking my head. I really didn't think it would be much of a trouble except for the number.

"I'll feed them, then yuh can take them out in the mornin'," said the hostler at the livery.

My foot was up on the lower rail as I watched the horses, large, beautiful animals, then turned my attention to the other corral, the one with the mules.

Stepping down, I turned to the hostler. "You know of anyone that would like to help me trail them to Durango?"

"Yuh might git ol' Phillips to help, if'n he ain't frozen to death," he responded.

He must have seen the puzzlement on my face. "What I mean is that he has a tendency for the bottle an' may have fallen asleep in an alley. That'd freeze him for sure last night."

I didn't want to deal with no drunkards. In my time I'd seen some who could handle their liquor and show up for work, but I've seen more that were a liability to a crew.

"Anybody else?"

"Couple of Ute youngsters that hang around sometimes," he paused, but those Injuns could just kill yuh an' steal them horses."

"They happen to be around?" I questioned.

"Don't know, don't care, an' haven't looked. Does that answer yur question?" he smarted. It almost made me want to thump him on the head, but I refrained.

I looked at him frowning. "Any more suggestions?"

He was shaking his head holding his chin in one hand. "Most riders have headed south or taken a job for the winter. Yuh might try the saloons."

"If you think of anyone or see those Utes around let me know. I'll either be at the eatery or the hotel," I told him before walking back toward my room.

I wasn't real concerned about the horses I just didn't know how they would mix with the mules. Mules can be downright cantankerous if they take a mind.

The day passed slowly. I didn't really mind staying over an extra day, but there was nothing for me to do. I walked up one side of the street and down the other for entertainment. I wasn't much for cards nor the atmosphere of saloons. There was a billiard parlor, but I wasn't much of a player.

I went back to the hostler in the afternoon. He was sitting in his small shack with the stove blazing. "Thought of anyone?" I inquired.

"Nope, nearly a soul," he said. "And I've 'most worn my brain out tryin' to think."

"How about a vaquero? There are plenty of Mexicans in town," I suggested.

He squinted his eyes. "Most of the men work the farms in the Valley. If'n there's a vaquero they'd be down in New Mexico or over in Texas. They don't like ridin' in cold weather."

The next morning I arrived at the corrals just as graylight was appearing. Approaching I saw the form of a man looking out over the corral. He turned my direction when I reached him.

"Heard you were lookin' for some help drivin' horses," he uttered with a hoarse voice.

I had seen some rugged-looking men in my time but he would be hard to beat. The heels of his boots were run down, the pants were put together with patches. I had no idea what kind of shirt he had as it was covered with a dirty blanket made into a poncho. On his head, well, he had something that once may have been a hat. The brim was partially torn off the right side.

He looked worn and bedraggled. The hair from under his hat was matted. The beard needed trimming and it looked as if a mouse had made a home in it.

"Name's Phillips, Gordon Phillips," he informed me reaching out his hand.

Phillips—the bum, the drunk. I recalled what I had been told about him. I did shake his hand then he attempted to straighten up.

"I know mules and horses," he stopped looking out at the horses in the corral. "I ain't never worked with draft horses before, but I'm willin' to give it a try."

Well, I hadn't worked much with them either, but I wasn't about to tell him that. I could use the help, but I was surely reluctant to take him on.

I decided to get right to the issue. "Phillips, I hear you're a drunk."

He licked his lips and ducked his head slightly. "Rightly informed," he replied. "But I ain't drunk now, and I need a job."

"Why, so you can buy booze and drink yourself into a stupor?" I snapped, not too kindly.

Lifting his head and straightening his shoulders, "I don't drink when I'm in the saddle!" he proclaimed.

I looked him over again. I believe in giving a man a chance. "That your nag over there?"

"Maybelle's her name. I wouldn't say she's a thoroughbred, but I wouldn't say she's a nag. In fact, I resent that. If'n yuh don't want me along, just say so."

Moving toward her, I asked, "Mind if I check your gear?"

"Mister!" he exclaimed. "I done told yuh that I don't drink when I'm workin'. There's no bottle!"

I stopped then turned to look at him. It was light enough now to see his face as he was looking toward the east. "You're hired. Twenty dollars paid when we get to Durango."

A smile lit on his face, he licked his lips again and held out his hand to shake confirming the deal. I held back. "There are two conditions. First, you'll clean up before we ride into Durango. I don't want you havin' all the dogs runnin' after you. Second, if I happen to find a bottle, or see you drinkin' on the trip I'll beat you so bad that even your mother wouldn't recognize you...not that she would anyhow." Then I thrust out my hand to shake his.

Glancing at his gear I asked, "You got a coat? It'll be cold up in the high country."

He tugged on his poncho. I've a couple more of these tied behind the saddle. Then he gave me a smile that was minus a front tooth.

"Let's get this show on the road," I prompted going over to mount Toit. Looking at the man walk to his horse, I began to shake my head. *What in the world had I got myself into*?

CHAPTER 28

The horses were ready to go, they didn't mind the trail, but we had to work some to get the mules moving. They tended to like the comfort of the stable and corral and didn't relish the thought of going up into the cold of the high country.

Phillips took his whip and cracked it over the ear of one of the mules. I watched him as he worked the whip over their heads and just to the back of their hindquarters. I'd seen some folks use whips before and he was as good as any. It made me think of what might have caused him to go to the bottle.

We worked them along the road, and I was thankful that there was no traffic save for a rider or two. Even with the pass open, but with folks knowing that a storm could rise at any time, they were satisfied with making do with what they had.

It took us a full day to get up over the pass. It was cold and spitting snow. Only a trail was being used but the horses moved right along. The mules hesitated at first, but with Phillip's whip and watching the horses, they followed. They almost had to as there was no place to turn back until the summit was reached.

We didn't bother to stay in Pagosa Springs and drove the herd right on down main street. The snow was falling steadily when we made camp that night. Looking back toward Pagosa, the road was hard to see and the mountains completely covered in clouds. It wasn't real cold, but that could mean an abundance of snow.

The horses and mules were tied to a rope corral. We let them graze before tying them up but they'd have to wait until morning as we kept them on a close tether.

Both Phillips and I collected wood. It was plentiful where we stopped, and we wanted to make sure we had enough to keep the fire going in case the snow began to fall harder.

I was making the coffee and Phillips had secured his bedding underneath a large blue spruce. We hadn't talked much on the trip being too busy during the day and too tired at night. I kept a close eye on Toit and he seemed to be doing all right.

After I opened a can of beans I left them next to the fire on a rock to warm. No use dirtying up a pan for them. Bacon and some fry bread would be the rest of the gourmet meal along with a pot of coffee.

It didn't take long for us to chow down. I had rinsed the skillet in the little stream and was coming back to camp when Phillips asked, "Were yuh in the War?"

I sat the skillet next to the fire, then picked up my cup to refill it, then I looked at him and nodded. "Fought in the Shenandoah Valley."

He became silent and seemed to withdraw somewhere within himself. I held the pot out and he reached out his cup for me to fill it.

After he took a sip he looked around, the snow had stopped falling. "Beautiful country," he said. "I was at Gettysburg and then fought across the mountains from you all the way to Appomattox," he paused for several moments. I didn't see a need to reply. "Don't know how I survived... Many a good man didn't."

I didn't figure he fought for the Union, "Where you from?" I inquired.

"Not far from Knoxville. I started out with Stonewall, but with the casualties I ended up with Bobby Lee by the end of the war."

"It was indeed terrible," I said in a whisper.

"Now...I live mostly in alleys or barns," he murmured. "Live from bottle to bottle wondering," he stopped to look up at me. "Mr. Forrest, I fight that war most every night. 'Bout the only time I don't is when I'm workin'."

I wiped my moustache off with the cuff of my coat. "Gordon," I used his first name. "You're alive because God's not through with you."

He gave a grunt, but I continued. "If the only time you're not relivin' that terrible ordeal is when you're workin', then I'd say you need to get a steady job."

Looking at me it seemed he wanted to say more, but instead threw the dregs of the coffee on a rock next to the fire that was hot enough for it to sizzle. He got up and walked to the spruce where he had laid out his bed.

The next morning, thank the Lord, the snow had stopped, and there was a hint that the sun might break through the clouds. It was the first time I had to wake Phillips up. He normally rose when I did.

I added wood to the coals and soon had it flaming, then put on the coffeepot. "Let's go!" I hollered. "Coffee's boilin' and I'm puttin' the bacon on."

There was a groan from his bedroll. I shut my eyes, praying and hoping that he hadn't a bottle hid. I wasn't feeling up to giving him a beating.

He sat up, I could see from his bloodshot eyes that he'd had a rough night. I didn't smell any liquor for which I was thankful. "Best be getting' out of that soogan," I paused and smiled. "If'n you don't soon I'll fill it with snow."

I went back to the fire and started cutting bacon throwing the slices into the skillet. There was a groan from the spruce then Phillips appeared. He stumbled my direction and I was afraid for a moment he might fall into the flames.

"Coffee," he muttered.

I didn't bother to look up, just answered, "You've got two hands, pour it yourself."

He knelt down on both knees, picked up the cup from the ground where he left it the night before, then shook it out. After he poured his coffee he held it in front of him and the pose reminded me of a person praying.

Slurping the coffee, he spoke, "Rough night. Don't usually have nightmares when I'm workin'."

"Mr. Forrest, I'm goin' to have to leave yuh when we get to a settlement."

"Name's Miles, and you can't. You made a bargain with me. You don't leave until the job is done."

He began to shake his head, the shaggy hair covering his face. "I can't," he wailed. "I can't," then he bowed his head sobbing.

I placed the skillet to the side where the bacon wouldn't burn, then placed my hand on the shoulder of Phillips. "Lord, help this man. Heal the hurt that is etched in his mind," I prayed. I could have said more, but sometimes its better to be silent and let the Lord do His work.

Phillips stayed bowed for several minutes, then straightened wiping the tears from his eyes with his dirty poncho. "Think I'll have some more coffee."

While we were eating I spoke. He hadn't said anything about what had happened. I reckoned he was some embarrassed. "I figure we're three days from Durango. There's a little settlement a day's ride from Durango. I expect you to clean up there."

Two days later we rode into a small village. For the last day we had been riding easy, the road was open, and if we needed to move off, the fields were open. I looked at the corral at the livery and figured our little remuda would fit in it rather easily.

The hostler didn't have a problem with us placing our animals there as there were no others with him right then. "To hay them will cost fifty cents an animal," he remarked.

"That's kinda steep, ain't it?" I said in mock surprise. I knew he was trying to make some money off me.

He shrugged, "Take it or leave it," then started to walk away.

"How about twenty dollars for all of them?" I asked.

Looking at the horses and mules in the corral, then at our horses. "Fifty cents per animal—final."

Well, if they were my animals I'd go on out of town. There was plenty of open ground with grass available under the snow. I hated to spend that type of money, but after all it was Kohlmeyer's.

"You got a deal, if we can stay in the barn," I told him.

He looked skeptical, and I thought he was going to charge us so I said, "We don't eat hay."

That brought a chuckle from him. "All right," he uttered, then looked at Gordon. "Payable in advance."

I looked at him, "What happens if those mules don't eat that hay?" I asked unbuttoning my coat to reach for my money pouch.

"Mister, I'm not going to stand out here in the cold to haggle with you," he snapped.

I dug out the money placing it in his outreached hand. He smiled then gave a slight nod. "One more thing. Anyplace a person can get a haircut and shave around here?"

The town was small, a saloon, livery, general store, and feed store. The town catered to the small ranchers in the area, and possibly a few miners, but it was away from the mining region.

He was jingling the coins in his hand, "Tim Denton, the barkeep has a place where you can get cleaned up. If'n he's not busy, he'll shave and clip you. Most likely you can get a bit to eat as well."

CHAPTER 29

I almost dropped the spoon into the bowl of chili I was eating. Phillips came out of that bath house all clean, shaven, with a fine looking haircut. The clothes I purchased for him at the little store while he was bathing fit him just about right. I couldn't believe it was the same person.

He walked over to my table with a grin spreading from ear to ear. "Hard to recognize me, Boss?" he said with a laugh. "I know, I don't even recognize myself."

My eyes kept wandering over him, I was really in surprise. "Sit yourself down, the chili's not the best, but it's fillin'."

Pulling out a chair he plunked himself down in it. I motioned for the bartender to bring him something to eat and in a few seconds there was a large bowl of chili in front of him.

"I'll pay you back for the clothes. I haven't felt so light in years, I reckon those old clothes have picked up a lot of mud and dirt," he said, then brought a spoon of the chili to his mouth. He tasted it, gave a small grimace, then continued to eat.

I just sat there watching him. After that first little expression, he must have changed his mind about the food for he surely gobbled it down. Lifting up the bowl toward the bar, I saw the bartender nod then came to get the bowl for a refill.

A minute later he came back with another full bowl. "Can I get you gents anything else? Tell you what, I'll even give you a drink on the house."

Gordon began to lick his lips and I knew it wasn't from the spice in the chili. "No, this'll be fine. How much do I owe you?"

Placing his chin in his left hand I saw him moving the fingers on his right as he was calculating the total. "Four bowls of chili, that's forty cents, a bath, shave and haircut would normally be thirty-five cents, but I'm going to have to charge a nickel more for the extra work and clean up," then he began to laugh. "I'm burning his old clothes and poncho as we speak. They were loaded with vermin."

"Here," I responded, pulling out my coin pouch giving him two dollars. "Thanks, he looks good on the outside, now to get him cleaned up on the inside."

The bartender smiled when I gave him the money, but it turned to a scowl. "What do you mean, 'cleaned up on the inside'?"

"Well, he like all mankind, needs to have his heart cleaned, be born-again like the Good Book says."

He kinda jerked back, "You a preacher?"

"No, but I know the Lord, and I know what He expects," I replied.

Gordon finished and we bid our goodbye to the bartender. When we hit the cold air, I noticed him fingering the collar of his new sheepskin coat. When he saw that I was watching him, he grinned.

We mounted to ride the little distance back to the livery. After caring for our horses we put our bedding down into the hay. The hostler had forbidden we make a fire in the barn, but it would be warm enough.

"One more day," I mentioned.

"Miles," he said in an almost whisper. "What'll I do when I get to Durango? You said yourself that places aren't hiring."

I was a mite concerned about that myself. If Gordon wasn't working, he'd go right back to the liquor. "Depends on you, I reckon."

There was no response so I continued. "You can go back to your old ways and haunts, or you can do what I said in the saloon—get your heart cleaned up."

"Will that mean that I won't drink anymore?" he asked excitedly.

I didn't want to blow smoke in his hope, but I couldn't lie to the man either. "Not necessarily. Sometimes the urge to drink will be gone, but for most folk it takes a matter of the will. However, sayin' that, I will add that the Lord will be with you helpin' you."

He didn't reply so I snuggled down in the hay. Soon I heard him snoring.

* * * *

A month later I was riding shotgun messenger on the stage to Cortez. Tom Larson had taken some time off to go visit family in Denver. The teamster next to me was humming a song he had just learned, his name—Gordon Phillips.

He accepted the Lord in the dirt of that barn floor the morning after his haircut and shave. As far as I knew, he hadn't touched a drink.

Bells McGinnity, had come down ill. He was the regular driver. He had some kind of fever and the stage office didn't want him to be around paying customers. I convinced them, with the help of Jim Hill, to give Gordon a try. I wasn't sure he could handle a six-team, but I know he could handle a whip.

On the regular run to Cortez and then on up to Utah the stage only used four horses. I figured that Gordon could handle them.

It had been a while since I rode the stage and the road was clear, so we had five passengers aboard plus Wells Fargo was sending a strongbox to the bank in Cortez. From what I could hear the passengers were on their way to California.

We were about half-way between Mancos and Cortez, a few miles north of those ruins they were calling Mesa Verde, when on the road in front of us were three desperadoes. If it had not been dangerous it would have been comical they way they looked.

I had the Greener in my hands when they stopped the stage. Gordon wanted to rush on by them, but I convinced him to stop as they might fire and hit one of the passengers. They told me to throw down my shotgun, instead I raised it up. My, were they novices at this.

"You boys do this often?" I asked as the three of them were together, right in front of me. I could hit two of them with one shot and then use the other barrel on the third one.

"Quit jabbering and throw down that shotgun!" one ordered waving his pistol around. "Tell the passengers to file out of the stage."

"Boys," I replied. "No one is getting out of this stage. Now judgment is waiting to meet with you, but I ask, are you ready for the judgment? Why don't you just put those pistols back in your belts and ride on out before you end up in the fiery pit?"

One of the riders began to back up, but the one doing the talking was flustered. He didn't want to be shamed. I watched his eyes then noticed his thumb moving to the hammer. Poor kid, his gun wasn't even cocked.

"I can see that you are all dangerous desperadoes, but you touch that hammer, you and your friend next to you are dead." The one rider had now backed on down the road. The other two decided that they would also heed my warning and started to ride away. I put down the Greener and pulled my pistol. Sure enough, the kid just couldn't stick to good wisdom. He stopped a few yards down the road, turned and took a shot. I fired twice, both bullets hitting him in the side.

He fell from his horse and I climbed down from the stage and went to him. He was blubbering like an idiot. After examining him I reckoned he would be seeing an earthly judge before he stood before his Maker. Will they never learn?

Gordon helped me load the kid to the top of the stage and tied him down so he wouldn't fall off. From the murmuring I could tell that there were a couple in the stage that were upset with me. A lady, middle-aged, whatever that is, kept going on about how I shot that boy.

Looking at her, I said, "Ma'am, I surely did. I have found in my experience that it is best to do so when someone is shooting at me." My answer didn't seem to register with her.

It was a full day before we arrived in Cortez with the boy unconscious most of the time. When he wasn't, he was groaning and moaning.

Gordon drove right up to the marshal's office. A man and the woman jumped right out and told the marshal to arrest me. She began to ramble on how I had shot the poor boy. I let her keep squawking for a while. The marshal looked at her and the man, then at me, then over to Gordon.

After the story was told, the marshal took the woman by the arm leading her away from the stage. "Ma'am, Mr. Forrest was acting in the line of duty," he spoke calmly and quietly.

Before she could answer, he took a step toward us. "I don't recognize him. You said there were three?"

I told him what happened with the other two, and how this one followed, then stopped to shoot at me.

The marshal was nodding his head, then left the lady standing there who had just been joined by the man from the stage. He grabbed a couple of by-standers to haul the kid off to the doctor's office.

CHAPTER 30

The stage company must have liked what they saw in Gordon for they hired him to run the stage from Durango to Pagosa Springs and back. Bells was back on the job, and even though old, he could still drive a team of horses. He resumed his old position. Larson was back from his visit so I was out at Wells Fargo and again unemployed.

I had taken to spending my time at the little diner. There was a table that I laid claim to as my own. It was in the center back of the room, next to the stove where on top was always a coffeepot. I liked to sit there, enjoy coffee, once in a while have a piece of pie, and watch Molly sway through the room waiting on customers.

They were now serving breakfast, but with a limited menu—biscuits and gravy, and you could buy an egg if you didn't mind it on top of the biscuits, which is what I preferred anyway. Currently they didn't have the money to purchase any new plates or cups. For some reason the bank didn't trust them with a loan; it sort of irked me some.

One morning I was sitting there; Helen and Molly were with me for a while as they had no customers after the morning rush, when Jim Hill came in and approached me.

"Mornin', Miles. Mind if I sit?"

I pointed to a chair and he pulled it out to sit across from me. Molly came to take his order—coffee and butterscotch pie. I had to smile, there was a man after my own tastes.

"Perhaps this isn't the best place to do business, but I have a proposition for you," he said as Molly came with his coffee.

He took a sip of the hot coffee, then wiped his moustache off with the back of his hand. I was waiting to hear what he had to say.

"I've been notified that I can offer you a job as a Wells Fargo detective," he said then forked a piece of pie into his mouth. He chewed a bit, then swallowed. "Wells Fargo is expanding its operation to southern Colorado and into Utah."

"Go on," I said now with interest. I looked up to see Molly standing a few feet away with the coffeepot in her hands—listening.

"With so much gold and silver coming out of the region they felt they needed an agent here in case problems arose," he paused for a minute to look at me. "There may be times when you'll have to travel as far as Salt Lake."

I nodded at Molly then held up my cup. She filled it and I rewarded her with a smile. "What exactly would be my duties?"

"At times you may ride along to help guard a large shipment or payroll, but mostly around in case something happens, such as a hold up. Then your job would be to bring the miscreants to justice," he informed me.

Holding the hot coffee in my hands, I thought for a minute before taking a sip. Then I felt Molly's hand touch my shoulder. I looked up at her, then back to Hill. "I'll take it, but I can't start for a week or so; I need to ride over to Rico to check on some friends."

I got a wide grin from Hill then he started to shake his head. "Don't you even want to know what it pays?"

"Jim, I know the job is for me," I told him, then put a hand on my chest. "I feel it here."

"You're on the payroll as of today," he said then held up his hands. "Don't worry, go see your friends, but while you're in Rico, stop in at the Wells Fargo office and introduce yourself. In fact, if the road is open to Telluride do the same there."

He had finished his pie, so he grabbed the cup and drank down the last swallow. Laughing a little he got up and started to walk away, then hesitated turning partway to look at me. "Oh, the pay will start at seventy dollars a month." Tipping his hat at Molly he went on out.

"That's wonderful, Miles!" exclaimed Molly. She took the chair where Hill had been sitting. We stared at each other for a few moments.

"Molly, I..." then customers came through the door before I could finish my sentence. She reached to touch my hand before getting up to wait on them.

The weather was nice the next morning with the sun breaking through the clouds. It was still chilly, but the temperature was above freezing. I saddled Toit and started on the road to Rico. I wanted to check on the Innesbergs, see how they were making out over the winter.

Instead of stopping to camp along the road I decided to spend a little money and stay at hotels along the way. The road was a little sloppy, but I pushed Toit a little so I could stay the first night in Mancos. It was a growing farming community.

I hadn't thought about it, but I could have taken the train from Durango to Dolores, the place I stayed the second night. However, I enjoyed riding in the saddle and taking my time to view and study the country. That's hard to do from a train coach.

From Dolores, the road would start traveling into the high country. The road was good, except in spots like the place where the Innesbergs had the accident. There were a few small ranches along the way where I figured I could spend the night in the barn.

The road followed the Dolores River all the way to Rico. There was still plenty of snow in the shadows of the canyon, but nothing plentiful on the road. It was the last day of travel before reaching the Innesburg ranch that Toit stopped on the road snorting.

I couldn't see what he was looking at as a mist was coming up off the river. When it passed I saw three riders on the trail. They were a tough-looking crew, and I could sense evil. It gave me an eerie feeling that caused me to shiver. The riders looked grisly, their faces like leather stretched taut over bone, their eye sockets deep-set in their heads. The horses upon which they were mounted were vicious, baring their teeth. I noticed that their sides were scarred from the riders raking them hard and deep with their spurs.

Nudging Toit forward, I could tell he didn't want to go. The riders didn't move, blocking the road. As I approached, blank stares came from hollow eyes looking at me, seemingly looking into my soul. I shivered again.

Something inside me said that they were of the Deceiver. As Toit approached the black horse reared and bared its teeth at Toit. "Get out of the way!" I hollered. "Now!"

I reached out grabbing the reins of the black horse from its rider's hands. It reared again, and I saw surprise in the rider's face as he grabbed for the saddle horn. I spurred Toit causing him to jump forward and we went between the riders of the red and black horses. The rider of the greenish colored horse, the pale horse, just sneered as we went past.

I could smell them as we rode by, the smell of dead flesh rotting. I could feel their cold, deadly eyes on my back as Toit was now walking down the road. Not looking back, I applied the spurs again and Toit put a little hurry-up in his gait.

We went around the bend for several hundred yards before I pulled Toit off the road to rest. I needed a break and reckoned he did as well. We walked down to the water's edge where I let Toit drink.

What I saw I knew wasn't real...or was it? I had read the Good Book where it spoke of the Horsemen in Revelation. I hit the side of my head a couple of times to make sure I wasn't hallucinating. The spirit within me was agitated, so I breathed a simple prayer of "Lord, help me."

That's all it took. I felt a peace return to my soul. I let Toit browse some, then drink again before mounting and heading on up the road.

Several hours later we were approaching Rico. I didn't bother to go into town as the turn off to the Innesberg's was this side of the town. Toit took me right up to the cabin. I looked around and was somewhat dismayed. George must not have gotten much stronger for there was little work done around the place. Someone was living there for I saw that the wood pile was somewhat depleted.

Dismounting I went up to knock on the door and was surprised when it opened immediately. There was a middle-aged woman with a fierce, yet scared look in her eyes.

"Whatdya want?" she snapped.

"I'm looking for the Innesbergs," I replied as politely as I could.

"Don't know 'em, now get 'way!"

I didn't bother to reply. Mounting Toit I rode to Rico going straight to Barney Callahan's store. I figured if anyone would know what had happened he would.

When I entered, I saw him look at me trying to remember who I was. Then he smiled coming to me with hand outstretched. "Miles Forrest, I remember you."

"Mr. Callahan," I said returning his handshake. "I'm lookin' for two of my friends and their children— the Innesbergs."

"Yes, nice folks," he sort of muttered. "They left about a month ago. From what I understand packed up personal belongings and left everything else behind."

I decided to go on down to the saloon to get a bite to eat. If I remembered right they had pickled eggs and sandwich makings.

As I entered I moved slightly to my left so I could survey the room before going any further and to allow my eyes to adjust. My eyes saw four men sitting at a table toward the back corner. Two were drinking, two were not.

Taking a deep breath I advanced toward the men at the table. Three I recognized, one was the profane kid, Loyal Reems, the other Amos Yarnell. The third man sort of surprised me.

"Lot Smith, what are you doin' here?"

He looked up and I saw a brief smile. I had met him a few years back up in northern Colorado and we spent time working and talking horses. I nodded at Yarnell, but ignored the other two.

"I'm lookin' for my friends, George and Catharine Innesberg and their two children. They had a small place just outside of town."

"Nary an idea," blurted Reems.

I was in no mood for games. "I think you're a liar," I challenged.

He jumped up to confront me. "Smith, tell this clown to sit down."

Smith reached over to grab him by the gunbelt. "Sit down, kid, before it's too late."

Reluctantly Reems took his seat. "Miles, I'd like for you to meet Zeb Imoft."

It was taking me a while to process what was going on. Lot was trying to warn me of something.

"Miles, the Bishop decided he didn't want the woman as his wife and had us encourage them to move elsewhere, away from the region," he said the hesitated looking toward the entrance. "This town along with Dolores will soon be a haven for the Chosen in southern Colorado. I assure you they were not hurt, they went back to their home, I think it was Ohio.

Lot wouldn't lie, at least I didn't think he would. Tell Hanks and the Bishop that I might ride their way sometime," I said, then started to turn.

"You'll never see Brother Hanks," screeched Imoft, kicking his chair away and pulling his gun.

We were too close. Then Imoft slumped to the floor. Yarnell had clobbered him on the head with his pistol. I looked at Smith and he smiled holding his dgun against Reem's ribs.

I tipped my hat, "Thanks," then moved away from the table.

"Miles, come join me on a hunt. I'm moving my family down to southern Utah. There's plenty of wild horses."

"Good health to you, Lot...Yarnell," I said then left the saloon.

CHAPTER 31

Riding out I figured Lot Smith was telling the truth about the Innesbergs, but perchance my trail came across Hanks, or even Bishop Malone I would sure bring the subject up. I would hate to see the Innesbergs fall into the hands of those so-called Zionists.

I rode about an hour before finding a place to camp next to the river. In my mind there was no need not to have a fire and make coffee, so after I took care of Toit I got a fire started and put coffee on to boil. Since I didn't have a chance to eat in Rico, I made some fry-bread and bacon.

There was a lot on my mind as I got down in my soogan for the night. I thought about the Innesbergs, and prayed for their best. But what weighed most heavily on my mind were those three horses and their riders I met along the trail.

Was it an omen? Then perhaps I was just imagining it, but no, Toit reacted to them as well. A glimpse into the spirit world maybe.

It was cold when I woke up the next morning. Quickly I got a fire started and when I went to make coffee, I found that there was ice in the pot from the coffee remnant from the night before. The sky was clear, but it was cold. I fried the rest of the bacon, after the coffee started to boil.

Within thirty minutes we were back on the road heading home to Durango. "Home," that word stuck in my mind when Toit stumbled. He gained his footing then lunged forward and started to fall. I kicked the stirrup loose, but was not fast enough to get out of the saddle and found myself pinned under Toit.

He lay completely still. My good horse, my friend since the War, was dead. I had ridden him many a mile. We'd seen some times together, been through some country. I'd surely miss him.

I knew he had been struggling with something recently, but I didn't think he'd fall dead alongside the road. Reaching over I patted him on the neck then remembered my predicament. I attempted to pull my leg out, but couldn't budge it. From my position I couldn't begin to lift Toit off my leg.

Laying there I began to ponder my situation. If I recalled right, there was a shack down the road a piece. The Greener was beside me, but I didn't think it would be much good, then I saw the rifle in the scabbard. Stretching I was able to grasp it and pull it out.

I fired three shots, then lay back down to rest. A few minutes later I leaned forward, firing three more shots. My leg wasn't hurting, but I could feel it going numb.

It was perhaps ten minutes later that a man and a boy happened upon me.

"Senor, you have trouble, si?" he asked in slurred English with a smile on his face.

"Si," I said returning the smile. "*Por favor,*" I pleaded pointing at my leg.

The man went across from me bending over to grasp the saddle horn. "Tomas, get down, you push."

With a grunt from the man they were able to raise Toit just enough so I could jerk my leg clear.

Stomping it on the ground, I was happy that it wasn't twisted or broken. Then I looked down at Toit. I'd never thought about burying a horse before; that would be a mighty big hole. A thing like that just never entered my mind.

"Guess it's better this way ol' boy. I hear back East, when a horse can no longer pay for its found they actually send them somewhere and make paste out of them. That's not goin' to happen to you."

The man and boy were standing there listening to me talk to a dead horse. "Senor, what happened?"

Sighing I looked over at the man, "Heart attack, I reckon. He was gettin' up in years." Then I looked at the man, "Do you have a horse I could borrow? I'll pay."

"No horse, but mule and burro. Come to the house, mi esposa will put on coffee. Tomas, help him with his gear."

He started walking toward his house while Tomas and I struggled with the saddle. Eventually we were able to get it off. He took the bridle and gear while I hoisted the saddle.

The woman of the house was rather plump and seemed happy, humming as she went around the table filling our cups with the hot, black brew. It was strong, but I liked it.

When I thanked her saying that it was very good, her face lit up with a large smile. I turned my attention to the man. "Senor..."

"Alfredo," he told me. *"Esta es mi esposa, Sofia, y mis nombre es Alfredo."*

I nodded. "Alfredo, I'd like for my horse to get buried. Don't want the varmints to get him."

He started scratching the side of his face. *"Gran hoyo,"* he replied.

Reaching in my vest pocket I pulled out my little pouch handing him two coins—a double and single eagle.

"*Demasiado,*" he stated, "too much."

"I need to borrow your mule as well. I'll leave it at the livery in Dolores."

He looked over at Tomas, who was nodding his head. "*Trato,*" he said reaching out his hand to sealed the bargain.

I went with them to the barn. The burro was definitely out of the question, but when I saw the mule my thoughts went back to the paste factories. That animal was so old and dilapidated, I didn't think it could make it to Dolores with me mounted on it.

A few minutes later I had the mule saddled and I mounted. Tipping my hat, "*Adios,*" then glanced back where Toit lay. I nudged my new mount and it started trotting over toward the road.

An hour later I found myself walking. That poor old animal couldn't handle my weight along with my gear. There wasn't much traffic on the road, but when any came by I ducked my head. I sure didn't want anybody seeing I was walking beside an old mule.

Fortunately the travel was all downhill and we were soon out of the heavy timber into a valley. The sun was shining bright, and if I hadn't lost Toit and wasn't leading an ol' mule, folks may think I hadn't a care in the world.

Trudging along, I had been walking close to ten hours. I saw a few small ranches along the way and was tempted to stop, but kept on moving. I was one tired ol' cowboy with sore feet when I saw the edge of town. I continued on up toward the livery. Needless to say I got my share of stares.

When I reached the livery a young lad ran out followed by the keeper. "You don't look like the kind that would ride a mule," he said.

"Not, that's why I'm walkin'," I replied with a smile. "Can I stow my gear here with the mule until I can find a horse. A Mexican boy, Tomas, will be by in a few days for the mule."

"Sure, sure," responded the hostler with a chuckle. I handed him two dollars.

Taking the money, he pointed toward the corral. "Just so happens, Saddleback has some horses in the corral out back. They probably would sell you one."

I wanted to take a break and clean up a mite, but figured I might as well go on back to see what they had. Did I mention plugs? They were maybe a step above the mules. Not the worst I'd ever seen, but I would sure hate to bet my life on one of them.

As I was standing there a Ute buck came up to me. "You the man who walks with a mule?" he asked.

I looked at him with a scowl.

"Don't buy horse here, come with me to village. We have good horses," and he took off walking.

Hesitating, I thought that he could be pulling a fast one on me, and my feet were already hurting, but I figured I should follow. Indians, especially Utes, know horses, but they could also be trying to get rid of some rank stuff.

Upon entering the camp he said, "Horses for sale, for right price. You lookum over."

It was a small village with a half dozen tepees. The children stopped playing when they saw me enter. I limped along with the young buck up to the make-shift corral. "Plenty good horses, you choose."

There were a dozen appaloosas and a few pintos hobbled around the cottonwoods. Now I normally prefer a solid color on a horse, but these animals looked good. Then the thought struck me that these horses may be stolen.

"Trade from Shoshone," the buck said, "Good horses. Sell you three for one hundred dollars gold."

"Three!" I exclaimed then turned to walk away.

He ran and grabbed me. "Look, you'll see." He pulled me toward the horses."

I knew of the Shoshone and their horses, and when I was working up in Wyoming I knew a couple of punchers who worked appaloosas. One thing for sure, they were very quick on their feet. They were never seen on the trail up from Texas which made me skeptical. Cowboys that worked them said they didn't see well in the dark, and that was vital on the trail.

Moving from one to another, I grunted a few times as I checked them over. He was right, this was prime horse flesh, but was I prepared to pay a hundred dollars? Once I had thought I'd like to raise horses, but now I had a job with Wells Fargo.

"Look at pintos, fine horses," he said motioning.

"From what I've heard and seen, I wouldn't give you two-bits for one of those painted horses, especially that skewbald. Tell you what," I hesitated sliding the toe of my boot back and forth in the dirt. "I'll give you the hundred dollars and you throw in that skewbald for two-bits, and it'll be a deal."

He looked down and I thought I saw a slight smile then reached out his hand. "Done deal."

"Ah, not so quick. I'm not givin' you money to spend on whiskey."

"No, me Christian Indian," he pointing toward a building. "Go to church, worship Jesus."

I then reached out to shake his hand. "Smart hombre. Done deal, now let's throw a saddle on this one."

"You want me to ride 'im?" he inquired.

I gave him a wry grin and put my foot in the stirrup. "When I can't ride one of these spotted cayuses, I'll take to the rockin' chair."

As soon as I hit the saddle he took off. Mercy me, if he wasn't trying to hit the moon. I wasn't expecting him to be half-broke. He jumped and turned, jumped some more, then stopped, plumb still. That did it, that stop—I flew off and felt the ground rise up to meet me.

It took my breath away, and I must have blacked out for a moment or two. I heard the hastening of moccasin feet my direction. When I looked up, I saw the young buck looking down at me disdainfully. "Maybe that the reason you walk with mules," he said with a smile. "There is a rockin' chair that the preacher uses over at the mission."

I grunted, dusted myself off a little. I was more than a little embarrassed for I had actually fallen off that horse not expecting him to stop suddenly like that. Mounting again I would be waiting for that trick.

"Yeehaw! Powder River let 'er buck!" That horse took off again. This time I stayed with him and when he took that sudden stop, I put a spur to his flank to get him bucking again.

When I wore him out riding him to a standstill, I dismounted with a smile. "That there horse is goin' to make me a good mount." I grabbed the Ute by the shoulder, "What's your name, my friend?"

"Red Hawk."

"Good name for that horse—Hawk. Now let's go up to the mission and write up a bill of sale."

CHAPTER 32

Once the passes were open Jim Hill rode with me to Silverton and over to Telluride to introduce me to the Wells Fargo people in the offices there. There was a small office in Rico, one even smaller in Cortez.

While in Rico I introduced Jim to Barney Callahan and his son Nathan telling him what good folk they were, and that Nathan was a sure enough hard worker.

It was still cold up in the high country so we made sure we had plenty of blankets to cover ourselves in the stage. I wanted to ride Hawk, but Jim said he preferred the stage, and he's the boss.

The mines weren't hiring yet, but it wouldn't be long. They never stopped producing, but they ran skeleton crews during the severe winter months.

Now that I was making regular wages, I would buy my meals at the eatery. They were tasty, but I enjoyed the company of Molly even more than the meals. Whenever I came back from one of those trips, she always had a piece of pie waiting for me.

But what did I have to offer? I was a cow-bum now turned stage-bum, I had nothing to offer Molly. I was moving around all the time, but then again, I wasn't just drifting. I'm not the type to settle down in a town, especially one that is growing like Durango and when they finished that railroad to Silverton, it would really take off. On the other hand, the ol' bones sure do feel the winters more than they used to. It was kinda nice to sit by the stove and drink coffee when I came in from a trip.

Two things happened at the end of February. The first was that Molly received a letter from Doc Shores. He said the new stove should be arriving the twelfth of March. That pleased her mother to no end.

The second was when Kohlmeyer came to visit while I was enjoying coffee at the eatery. He had been a gracious man to me. He told me that he had found a buyer and was selling out. That surprised me, before he said he would still be shipping on the train.

He was grumbling when he mentioned the train. It was his first thoughts that he would still control the shipping of goods, but found out it would be the railroad. They would use his warehouse, but they would get the profit from shipping. He said he could stay and ship to some of the small towns, but since he had a buyer he decided to sell.

I asked him what he was going to do? He said, "Going to California. I have a daughter out there and a couple of grandkids I haven't seen. Going to spend some time with them."

When I prodded him about work, he just said that he'd find something when he was ready. With the sale of the company he would have plenty of money in the bank. Which I knew he already did. He was not afraid to spend money or give to help a person, but he was also wise in how he did it.

I had just been out riding Hawk and had reined in at the eatery, when Gordon Phillips intercepted me before I could enter.

"Miles, I just came from the saloon," he began when I interrupted."

"Saloon! Gordon!"

"Easy, Miles, that's how I handle it. I stand outside for a few minutes, the temptation doesn't come and I just want to know I have the victory over the bottle," he informed me. "But I do have someone to show you."

He started walking toward the saloon with me right behind him. At the entrance he pointed out a kid playing cards that looked vaguely familiar.

"It's the outlaw you shot over by Cortez," Gordon said.

That didn't make sense. He should have been tried and sent to prison by now. Seeing him there I reckoned he had healed all right.

I spun on my heel and headed for the marshal's office leaving Gordon behind, but he soon caught up with me.

Conrad Belkins, the marshal, was a good man; I rode with him once. "Marshal, there's an escaped prisoner in the saloon," I hollered barging into his office.

"Easy Miles. If you mean Trundel, he was released."

"Released, on lack of evidence."

"Lack of evidence!" I exclaimed. "What about my deposition? Gordon's? The other passengers on the stage?

"It seems that there are conflicting opinions," responded the marshal.

I was a little exasperated. "Then it should be decided in court."

Belkins dropped his head for a moment, then I heard a voice sitting over in the corner. I hadn't seen him, or her, when I came in.

"Oh, Mr. Forrest, there will be a day in court," he mocked standing and handing me an envelope. "My name is William Thornton and this is my wife Marjorie. You may remember us from the stage in which the young man was viciously shot down."

I remembered my manners, so I nodded and tipped my hat to the lady, "Ma'am," but all I received was a snide smile. I remembered her all right.

Clearing his throat to get my attention, I looked at Thornton. "I represent a certain Adam R. Trundel of which these papers are issued to you, as he is bringing suit. See you in court, Mr. Forrest." He turned and walked out of the office; I received that same glib smile from his wife as she followed him.

I didn't know whether I wanted to thump him or lose my lunch. Eastern tinhorn litigator! I opened the envelope. "For the dangerous discharge of a firearm that brought injury to Adam R. Trundel thus keeping him from gainful employment."

"Conrad, this is nonsense," I snapped at the marshal.

"Things are changing, Miles."

I thrust the paper at him. "Truth and rightness, and justice do not change!"

He sighed, then said, "The judge will be in town for a week, then won't be back for a month. If I were you, I would try to get a hearing before he leaves. These things can be drawn out."

Picking the papers off the marshal's desk, I turned bumping into Gordon who had heard the whole thing. My first stop was to the telegraph office where I contacted Dave Cook, then over to see the judge. Then I went back to find Trundel. He wasn't at the saloon where I saw him before, so I started searching the other saloons and dives in town. I figured he would go to the shady part of town. I found him playing cards in a pit with an appropriate name – "Death's Door."

The punk kid who bungled the holdup job was playing with some down-and-outs, laughing and having himself a good old time. As I walked up his face turned pale when he recognized me. It wouldn't remain that way for long. I grabbed him by his shirt jerking him from the chair. Slapping him I said, "You're a two-bit liar and coward, Trundel," and I slapped him again.

I looked over at those playing cards with him, and they started shaking their heads letting me know that he wasn't with them. "I'm surprised you men let a bag of scum like this sit at your table." I slapped Trundel again then threw him against the wall. His face was now red with a mixture of embarrassment, rage, and the mark left by my hand.

"Bah!" I said in disgust, turned and walked away.

There was a blast from a shotgun. The bartender yelled, "Not in the back!" He had fired above Trundel's head.

I turned drawing my pistol. The kid had dropped and was now groveling on the floor, whimpering, begging me not to kill him. The men around were snickering at him and I nodded to the bartender. "I owe you."

Holstering my gun, I turned to leave and there he was, in the doorway, a certain William Thornton. I figured he must have followed me or was looking for Trundel himself...or was it a set-up?

The first words out of his mouth were, "You knocked my client to the floor. Harassment will be added to the charges at the hearing."

"He's on the floor 'cause he's a snibblin' coward; a rat looking for a hole to crawl into," I remarked. "And Mr. Litigator, I talked with the judge, the hearing will be day after tomorrow.

I could see the displeasure on his face. He was counting on having plenty of time to put his case together.

Gordon stayed in the dive while I went over to the eatery. I needed some coffee and good company. I didn't think about leaving Gordon in the midst of temptation, I was too mad.

As I approached I saw a young kid running toward me. "You Miles Forrest?" he asked. When I nodded he handed me a telegram that was from Dave Cook. I reached in my pocket pulling out a dime and when I handed it to him, I received the biggest smile. It made me feel good. I chuckled to myself. Sometimes the smallest things can help a person.

I waited until I was seated at the table with coffee in front of me to read the note from Cook. "Be in Durango tomorrow night—STOP--bringing lawyer Henry Evans recently of Kansas City."

"May I read it?" inquired Molly who was standing beside me. I handed her the telegram. "What's this about?"

Motioning to a chair she sat down with me and told her the whole story. "Well, it's good that your friend, Mr. Cook, is bringing a lawyer then. Are you concerned?"

I lifted my hands from my cup in a gesture that said I didn't know what to think. In my mind it was an open and shut case. What was happening to the law? Justice was being sabotaged by shyster lawyers.

CHAPTER 33

The next day Dave Cook arrived by train with a lawyer supplied by Wells Fargo. Dave introduced him to me, "Miles, this is Henry Evans, recently of Kansas City, but originally from Texas," he said with a smile. "He'll represent you, courtesy of Wells Fargo."

I reached out to shake his hand. Looking in his eyes it seemed like I knew him; there was something familiar about him. "I knew an Evans from Texas, Bass Evans."

A smile broke out on his faces, "He's my father."

"My mercy!" I exclaimed. "You're little Hank? Your father and I rode the trail together a few times. I remember see you when I stopped at his ranch. Why, you were just a little rascal. How is your father?"

"It's Henry now," he smiled with a little mock cough. "More lawyer-like than 'little Hank.' He's spoken of you often, Mr. Forrest, and to answer your question, he's living out his days in Wichita. Mother is able to take care of him for now. A horse fell on him a couple years ago; broke his hip and did something to damage his lungs. But they have a little house at the edge of town and are as happy as the situation allows."

"I'm really sorry to hear that. Bass was a good man to ride the trail with. And your Mom, Abby, isn't it? She could bake anything that had dough."

Henry chuckled, "I'll write them, and tell them I saw you. Now, let's go somewhere and talk about the case."

Entering the court the next day I had to smile. Trundel was sitting there with crutches by his side. He was going to soak up as much sympathy as he could. The Honorable Gideon Z. Jeremiah entered the court to preside over the hearing; he looked at me, then at Trundel, scowling. Immediately Thornton started.

"Judge, I must object. There are firearms in the room, one being carried by the defendant. He is a dangerous man of questionable character! I demand he be disarmed!"

"Mr. Forrest is an officer of the law as is Mr. Cook. Mr. Thornton, it is best you do not question a man's character until you know him. A man's character is vital out here in the West."

"Your Honor," said Evans. "Mr. Forrest will honor the request and remove his gunbelt. But this in only a hearing; I move that the case should not go to trial. Shots were fired at Mr. Forrest. In the completion of duties as..."

"I object!" Thornton shouted. "I was there and only one shot was fired. The one by Miles Forrest that injured Mr. Trundel as he was riding away."

I was holding my gunbelt in my hand, and as Thornton finished I sorta laid it heavily on the table. He jumped when he saw my Schofield, holstered, only a few feet from him.

"Your Honor," interrupted Evans. "This can be solved right now. Marshal Belkins is here, so is the doctor that took the bullets, notice I said bullets, from Trundel's leg. If Mr. Thornton was there, he was mistaken, for there was at least two shots fired by Mr. Forrest in discharge of his duty for the Rocky Mountain Detective Agency and Wells Fargo."

The Judge had the marshal and doctor verify this. Then he asked Gordon to describe what happened to which Thornton objected as he hadn't been sworn in. When Gordon was finished, Thornton stood up, "I call Marjorie Thornton to the witness stand."

"Sit down and be quiet, Mr. Thornton," the Judge advised. "I see no reason for your wife to perjure herself. Case dismissed as Mr. Forrest was in the process of carrying out his sworn duty."

I was buckling on my gun as we were leaving when we heard Mrs. Thornton scream and a loud thunk. Trundel had taken his crutch and smashed Thornton alongside the head, then swung hitting the bailiff. I saw him grab the downed deputy's gun. He pointed it at Thornton.

"You said we were going to make a lot of money off this deal," yelled Trundel.

I think Thornton thought his time on earth had run its due. I turned toward the two of them getting Trundel's attention. He turned the pistol toward me. Taking a step forward, I noticed his hand trembling.

"Put the gun down, Trundel, or you'll be the guest at another judgment in a few seconds."

It was then that Thornton moved causing Trundel to turn at the sound and fired. The bullet hit the floor next to where Thornton had been lying. I drew as Trundel turned toward me; when a shot came from the bench. Judge Jeremiah fired from a gun his had drawn shattering Trundel's skull. He fell directly on top of Thornton who gave a death-curdling yell that matched the one his wife gave out.

I nodded at the Judge, tipped my hat to Mrs. Thornton, and reached down to help the litigator up. I probably shouldn't have done it, but I got a big grin on my face as I turned my attention back to Mrs. Thornton. "You better get him back to your room so he can change his pants."

That brought a heehaw of laughter from Gordon, then we all left the courtroom.

* * * *

In a little house on the edge of Fifth Street men were lounging around, arguing, drinking whiskey, and making sinister plans.

"The payroll will be coming soon for the Iowa, Gold King, and Tiger mines," said a tall, lean man.

There was a grunt from a stocky rough-looking character, "Are you sure we can trust this Wiggins to get us accurate information?"

"He knows what will happen if he doesn't come through, Impson. What about that half-wit with you? I wouldn't trust him to find his way across the street," came the terse reply.

"Brit will do what I tell him. He can handle a gun and a knife. Ain't that right, Joe?"

The man he spoke to went by the name of "Curly" though his head was as bald as a baby's behind. He was a solidly built man, a little taller than Impson. The three of them had been involved in the holdup months back near Idaho Springs.

"Wish Cooke would have made it. He was a good man, fast with a gun," said Impson.

There came a grunt. "Must not have been too good, he's dead," sneered the leader.

Ezra Nation, gunman, killer for hire, robber, and wanted for murder in several states. He wasn't as well-known as the other desperadoes, but his name was feared along the outlaw trail.

"I'll go see Mad Dan Buckley tomorrow. He's been hiding up here in the mountains for several years. He rode with Anderson, then with Quantrill. That's where I met him," he said shaking his head. "Ruthless man, worse than Anderson and he would go on a rampage, that's why they called him 'Mad Dan.'"

"After this," started in Impson, "I think I'll settle down, maybe go to California."

"Pfft, you ain't got it in you to settle down. You're just like me. Lust for the fight, want to see that gold and silver, and it don't matter who gets in the way."

CHAPTER 34

Winter seemed to be on its way out, but of course, the high country could still get some storms. The days were warmer, the grass was growing and here and there one could see flowers beginning to bud.

Molly and Helen had fixed up the new diner nice. The stove had come in and they had it set up and working. With that, the bank saw fit to give them a small loan to get things started up again. They purchased new tablecloths either blue or red checkered, found some ornaments to put on the walls, purchased dishes and silverware. When a person entered, they received a real homey feeling.

I had been taking Hawk out almost daily to get him used to me. He wasn't fully broke and he sure enough was not the horse that Toit was, at least not yet.

It was mighty comfortable sitting at the table that I sorta claimed as my own, back next to the stove. There was a table of miners consuming some of Molly's pie. They would be heading up to the hills as the mines would be hiring full-time.

I finished one cup of coffee and was up at the stove where they kept a coffeepot. I refilled my cup then sat down. "Ahh, nice to be home," I said to myself. Home? It's been a long time since I called any place home.

The coffee tasted good, hot, black, and strong. Sometimes when it got to sitting on the stove too long it could get scorched. They must have made this pot just before I came in.

Through the door walked a man, maybe six foot tall, but very thin. He was dressed in black from hat to boots with silver conchos on his belt. Right off I didn't care for the looks of him. I know that some people say we shouldn't judge by first impressions, but it was easy to see that this man was evil.

He walked up to the table where I was sitting. "You're at my table," he growled.

Well, I had never seen the man before, and certainly not at this table. "That so?" I murmured and continued to sip my coffee.

"Out, now!" he barked.

I looked up at him wearily. This was a bad hombre, but I was tired and wasn't going to get up, especially for the likes of him. "Plenty of tables, sit at another one," I told him, not too friendly.

Then Molly bounded out of the kitchen. I noticed she was holding in her hands a plate with a piece of butterscotch pie. "I saw you come in and I wanted to bring you a surprise."

As she glanced at the man, the smile fell from her face. "Ezra?" The plate fell from her hands and smashed on the floor.

He laughed. "I bet you figured you would never see me again." He reached out to touch her hair. "Fact is, Molly dear. I'm looking for your father," he paused, then added, "then perhaps we can start our relationship anew."

I could see she was visibly shaken. "I, I don't know where he is. Not here for sure."

A sinister smile came to his face and he calmly said, "Molly dear," then quick as a flash he slapped her with the back on his hand. She was falling and would have hit the floor if I hadn't caught her. "Where is your father?" he asked sternly.

Placing her in a chair, I checked to make sure she wasn't hurt, then took a step toward the man. Molly grabbed me, "Miles, don't, please."

I looked at her, then back to him and saw that he had his gun out. He was fast, no way I could have matched that draw. I stared in his eyes and could see that he was ready, looking for any excuse to pull the trigger.

"No, Ezra. He's up in Silverton. I don't know where he stays," she semi-lied and I wondered what this evil man wanted with her father. She knelt down and began to pick up the broken pieces.

My eyes stayed on the man, who turned his attention to me, smiling. I trembled. I recognized that smile for I had seen it a thousand times in my dreams and other placed—it was the devil's grin.

"Another time," he told me with a wink. "Later," he said to Molly then turned walking out of the eatery. He stopped at the threshold, "Don't let me catch you sitting at that table again." Then looking over at the miners, he tipped his hat before walking outside.

I sat down, shaking my head. What had happened? Looking over at Molly she was trying to hold back the tears while cleaning up my butterscotch pie from the floor.

"Molly."

"Miles, don't, not now," she cried, got up and rushed to the kitchen.

My head was in a swirl. What in the world was going on? Who was this man Ezra? My thoughts were rushing through my brains like a stampede of thirst-driven longhorns to water.

In a few minutes she came back from the kitchen with a wet rag in her hand followed by her mother. Timidly she approached me. "Miles, that was Ezra Nation," he paused for a moment. "I knew him at another time in my life, back in Missouri."

My eyes went to Helen's. She seemed to be in a state of shock. Then I spoke to Molly, "What did he mean, start your relationship anew?"

She shiffled, then answered. "I was a young, infatuated young girl and not knowing any better I had a crush on Ezra. He was much older, but he had something about him, swagger, confidence, command." She saw me frown. "Miles, I was only ten. Nothing came of it."

"Miles, we're closing down early today. Mother and I need to talk," she said in a whisper. "Please understand."

Nodding I took that as my cue to leave. "Miles," she said. "You can't fix everything with a fight, with a gun. If you try it with Ezra, he'll kill you."

I smiled, "First thing, Molly, I'm a hard man to kill. Second," I paused, my smiled growing. "You're my girl."

With that being said I put on my hat, nodded toward Helen then turned to leave. "We'll talk tomorrow."

The next morning I went to talk with Kohlmeyer. He had found a buyer and said he would be moving out within the month. I hated to see him go, he had been such a friend. He said that he was looking forward to spending next winter in warm, sunny California.

Then he became serious. "Miles, I heard about that ruckus at the eatery. There's something more to it than you're seeing," he hesitated then smiled. "If you've any sand in yur craw, you'll save Molly from that fellow."

"Vern, he's fast, mighty fast," I replied.

"It don't always have to be with guns," he said, as he took off his hat to scratch the top of his head. "But if it comes to that, it comes to that. Never saw you for a quitter; didn't realize you'd scare that easy."

I dropped my head at the comment. "That's kinda low," I harped.

"You do what you're supposed to do, what you're called to do. You can keep your horses in the corral, but I need money for the found. You'll have to make a deal with the new owner when he comes 'round.'

The little pinto I purchased from Red Hawk when I acquired Hawk was a gift I planned on giving to Mollly. I decided to wait on giving it to her until I found out how this was going to play out. I needed more information on Nation, so I went to the telegraph office sending a wire to Dave Cook.

Stan Offut was the clerk in the telegraph office. He was a cordial little man, always polite. While working he always had on a pair of spectacles. I reckoned they helped him to read. His wife fit him. Stan was a little man, but his wife, though not tall was a little more stout. Whenever I saw them together they always seemed to be happy.

I told him I would be at the eatery and wanted an answer as soon as it came in. Then I strolled over for a late breakfast. If troubles were to come my way I might as well face them with a stomach full of biscuits and gravy. Upon entering I saw that the table I normally sat at was vacant, so I sauntered over to it.

CHAPTER 35

The eatery was half full when I entered. I went to "my table," and sat down. Molly was hustling around waiting on tables, refilling coffee cups and I just sat there enjoying watching her.

When she came to bring me coffee I saw quickly that she wasn't wearing her normal encouraging smile, but was somber. "Miles, it would be best if you would just leave."

I twisted at the end of my moustache then gave her my request. "I'd like some biscuits an' gravy with a couple of eggs on top, bacon, and, some pie on the side." Then I looked up at her with a cocky smile.

"Miles," she snapped, "this is no time for foolishness, it would be easier if you'd just leave."

Still smiling, I responded, "Thought 'bout it, but seems as if easy ain't in my make up. Not much in my life has come from easy, and I reckoned I couldn't live with myself by runnin' away. Plus, my guts tells me that there's more to this than I'm a-seein'."

"Miles, don't..." she started to say more but turned to take my order to the kitchen.

She had entered the kitchen when Tommy Fowler rushed through the door holding a scrap of paper in his hand. "This is for you, Mr. Forrest."

I reached in my vest pocket for my coin pouch pulling out a dime, flipped it to him and nodded. The dime was worth it for the grin I received. His mouth opened; a person might've thought I gave him an eagle. He scurried on out, looking at the dime.

Nation is sinister and deadly—STOP--he rode with Quantrill—STOP--no warrants in Colorado—STOP--known to visit mining towns will dig deeper. --Cook

I read the message over again; not very comforting. Was there something Dave was trying to tell me beyond what was written?

There was a swallow left in my cup and I found myself swirling it around when Molly came with my meal. After setting my food down she picked up the cup to fill it. She happened to come to my other side to set the cup down when I saw it.

"Come here, Molly," I ordered standing to my feet. I grabbed her by the arm so she couldn't run off and looked at the side of her neck—a bruise the size of a man's hand.

"Miles, don't," she sobbed.

"Did Nation do this?" She pulled away and rushed to the kitchen. I had my answer.

In my day I had seen some low-lifes; some downright mean people. Anyone who hits women or children are real close to the bottom; sit right next to the devil himself. Scum is too good a word for them. My mind was pretty well made up, but this clinched it.

Getting up I made my way to the kitchen. Molly was in her mother's arms, still sobbing. "What hold does he have on you?" I asked staring at Helen. She turned her face away, going to the stove.

I went to Mrs. Johnson and confronted her. "Not facing the truth is no good," I calmed down speaking softly, my hands holding to her arms. "Helen, let me help, where is he?"

Letting out a big sigh she said, "He said he was riding back to Silverton."

Releasing her, I moved a step back. "Silverton?" I muttered to myself. "Why?"

I went over to Molly. "I'll be back in a week," I said then started to walk away.

"Yes, in a pine box! Don't go Miles, he'll kill you!"

Stepping back to her, I reached to touch the bruise on her neck. She grabbed my hand, not to remove it, but to hold it against her. "Don't worry Molly. Some men take a sight of killin'. Besides I have a special present I need to give you when I get back." I smiled, then I saw the flicker of hope in her eyes.

Coming back into the dining area I saw that my breakfast was cold. I frowned, but picked up the bacon and started to eat it on the way out.
I went over to the office to talk with Jim Hill, letting him know what I was doing.

"I'll only be gone a week, most likely less," I informed him.

He was solemn. "Don't be gone any longer. We'll be shipping a payroll up there within the month."

"Jim, have you ever heard of Ezra Nation?"

When I mentioned his name he seemed startled. "Nation!" he exclaimed, then settled. "Why do you ask?"

"He's been in town and has been in Silverton," I paused to pull at my moustache looking into the eyes of Hill.

"You be careful, Miles," he stated, "And I want you back within the week." He turned his back going over to stand behind his desk.

I didn't reply, just went on out the door, but I knew the name "Nation" put him on edge.

In no time I had Hawk saddled, my gear loaded and ready to go. I was wearing a jacket but I tucked my heavy coat in with my bedding because cold weather could hit up in the high country. Pulling out the Schofield I checked the loads, then made sure I had a box in my saddlebags; then did the same with the Greener.

Mounting, I said, looking toward the base of the canyon. "Okay, Lord, yea though I walk through the valley of the shadow of death I will fear no evil." I smiled, "Thy Scofield and Thy Greener comfort me in the presence of mine enemies." Then I gave Hawk a nudge with my spurs and we were off.

The ride to Silverton proved uneventful, giving Hawk and I an opportunity to know each other. He seemed to understand that this wasn't a Sunday afternoon ride, but one with purpose. The nights in the high country were cold, and the second morning I wakened to a skim of snow on the ground.

Upon arriving in Silverton, I rode to Kohlmeyer's warehouse and store to find Johnson. There was still plenty of snow lying around, plus slush and mud. I was glad I didn't have to spend the winter up here.

Johnson was in charge of the warehouse and I was surprised he wasn't there. I went on into the store as I knew the proprietor always kept a pot of coffee on the stove.

Bing Miller greeted me with a smile and immediately offered me a cup and motioned to the chair by the stove. He was called "Bing" because of his bright cherry-looking cheeks. Always a cheerful man and we spent a while exchanging small talk—the weather, business, and Kohlmeyer selling out.

"Ever met a fella by the name of Ezra Nation?" I asked.

"Not that I recall, but with spring coming, there's lots of strangers moving in and out of the diggings right now. You might check in the saloons."

I nodded, then said, "You'd know him. Thin, a little taller than me, wears black and a nice-looking gun."

Bing told me that Johnson had a tent down in the little slum areas of tents. As he was speaking a horn blasted; it signalled the change of shifts at the larger mines. I thanked Miller for the coffee and the conversation then went out to head toward the haggard mess of tents.

The sixth tent down I saw Johnson out getting a fire going and preparing supper. With the traffic on this road it had turned into a quagmire. I walked Hawk up to his tent and waited.

He looked up then smiled. "Miles, light yourself! My goodness man, it's good to see you!" He hopped up and came to me and vigorously shook my hand. "Stay for supper. I'm getting the biscuits ready and I've got some slow elk and a pot of beans. We'll have a little feast. Go ahead, get down, and get yourself some coffee while I finish the fixin's."

Supper was fine, and sitting around the campfire after sipping coffee, I looked at Molly's father. "Tell me, Mr. Johnson, what's your connection with Ezra Nation?"

His face darkened and I could feel a sense of gloom come over him. "How do you know Nation?" he asked.

"Met him in Durango a few days ago. Seems like he has quite a hold on your wife and Molly." With that he dropped his cup and groaned. I continued to question, "Has he been here?"

"Oh, Lord, no," he groaned out loud. "Please God...don't let it be."

"Johnson! Get yourself together!" I commanded not expecting the outburst.

"Miles, it goes back to the War," he said softly, gaining his composure. "My name was known as 'Dan Buckley,' 'Mad Dan Buckley.' I was not Daniel Johnson then. I rode with Bloody Bill Anderson, then with Quantrill. Miles," he said dropping his head for a moment before continuing with sadness, "I was evil and did terrible, evil things. Nation was with Quantrill and we reaped havoc on anyone against us."

"I thought when I left the gang and the War was over that I could leave it all back in Missouri. I wanted to be a good husband and father. I started to attend church and became a Christian. Honestly, I repented of all those things I did, and we came West."

He sat there, picking up his cup wiping it clean. "Miles, I still have dreams of those years; I still see the faces."

"The devil's grin," I muttered interrupting him.

He glanced at me, then nodded. "While they called me 'Mad,' Nation was absolutely crazy. He loved to kill or maim—to cause pain."

"He's not contacted you?" I asked.

Shaking his head then placing his face in his hands he spoke, "Nation is not in Silverton."

"Get up, you're coming to Durango with me. Your wife and daughter need you there."

He started to protest when a shot rang out. Hitting somewhere between Johnson and myself. Then another shot, Johnson moaned and fell.

CHAPTER 36

There was virtually no cover so I hit the ground, trying to push my belly button deep into the earth. All of the trees had been cut for construction in the mines. We were out in the open.

I pulled my pistol out of habit, but figured the person doing the shooting was well out of pistol range. I kept waiting for another shot. Johnson was moaning some, but there was nothing I could do about that at the moment. I lay there, still as could be, my eyes scanning the hills. After fifteen minutes or so, I pushed myself slowly off the ground waiting for a slug to smash into me. When none came I went to see about Johnson.

The bullet had shattered his knee. "Guess that solves a problem. You're not goin' to be able to do much work for a spell. Now, no arguin', you're goin' down to Durango with me."

His groaning was becoming louder. He had to be in pain. "Is there a doc in the camp?" I inquired.

Between groans, he muttered, "There's someone who calls himself a doctor. Probably the best there is in Silverton, don't trust him none though."

I took his bandanna, sure didn't want mine covered with blood, and wrapped it around his knee. "I need to get that bleedin' stopped and get a splint."

Looking at the knee I didn't figure he would ever walk without a crutch or at least a cane again. His time working a claim was over. This was a bad situation, but I reckoned the Lord knows what to do with a bad situation.

The bleeding had stopped, but he was in terrible pain. "Let me go see about a wagon so I can get you down to the doc's."

I jumped on Hawk heading down the canyon. Johnson would have to deal with the pain until I got back.

It didn't take long. Bing had a wagon, he sent a man in the store to fetch the doc, then went with me to help with Johnson. When we arrived back at the camp, Johnson was half sitting up. His face was pale as one of the sheets at Laura June's boarding house where I stayed in Abilene.

"Hang on, Dan," came the steady voice of Bing as we hoisted him up into the wagon. He groaned louder and I thought he might pass out, which I reckoned might be a good thing. The jostling on this old muddy camp road wasn't going to do him any good.

It wasn't far, but from the sound of his moaning you'd a thought it was a hundred mile trip. A couple of men came out and helped us carry him into the doc's. As the doc cleaned the wound he grunted, hmmmed and hawed.

"Bullet's gone, but that knee is shot. Best I can do is splint it to keep it from moving and causing him more pain. I don't want a bone to break and cut an artery. That'd fix him for good," the good doctor informed us.

As the doc was splinting Johnson's leg, I asked Bing if I could borrow the wagon. He shook his head no, but that I could drive the load that was going down tomorrow.

I looked at the doc, who had finished splinting and was giving him a spoon of some liquid which I figured was laudanum. He answered my look, "Don't make any difference; one day, two days, a week. He's not going to be walking and it's gonna hurt no matter where he lies."

The next morning we woke to a heavy frost. Bing had moved a few things around in the wagon to help make a bed with a buffalo robe for a mattress and another one to cover him. When we loaded Johnson I gave him a spoonful of the laudanum. The doctor told me a spoon every four hours, no more.

Bing waved as we moved out back down the canyon toward Durango. "It was Ezra, wasn't it?" he asked.

"Don't know," I replied. "But reckon he is as good a suspect as anyone."

The laudanum had made Johnson groggy, and he soon was asleep. I rode with the Greener across my knees, but if he had a rifle there were a hundred places on the trail where he could pick us off. I was trying to figure out why Nation would shoot Johnson, it didn't make any sense, and from what I already knew about Ezra Nation, I didn't figure he wanted to kill us right off. He enjoyed inflicting the pain, and he had something else in his plans.

I was doing the best I could not to hit the rocks and ruts in the road, but there were still plenty. I think he must have moaned with every jolt. When I would stop for a break, I would have to lift him out of the wagon. At least Bing had found some old crutches in the store for him, but he still stumbled around.

The second night out I laid him down then put the coffee on and started to make supper. We traveled late and started early each day. I wanted to get him to Durango, but even so they were slow days.

He was ranting and groaning causing quite a commotion. I decided to check on his wound so I unwrapped the bandage. It didn't look good and I was afraid that gangrene was beginning to set in. The wound was bright red, and full of pus. I put my knife in the fire and told him to hold on that I was going to have to clean his wound. I squeezed on it, then took the knife and began to clean it. My mercy, he howled like a scalded Indian and kicked his leg around so that I was feared that I might cut him. I motioned for him to lean toward me, and then I walloped him and he went out. I needed to take care of this without him thrashing around.

I don't think it had started to rot, especially since he could feel the knife when I worked on him. He needed to see a real doctor. I didn't know what else to do, so I took a little of the bacon grease to smear it on the wound then wrapped it up with clean bandages.

"You didn't have to hit me," he groaned touching his chin.

"Didn't know what else to do as you wouldn't stay still and I was afraid I was goin' to do more damage with my knife. Seemed like the thing to do at the moment.

Reaching out I grabbed the new bandanna he was wearing and tied off the bandages with it. "Say!" he exclaimed, "Why don't you use yours?"

I pulled the knot tight and smiled. "'Cause the wound belongs to you. It wouldn't be fittin' if it was all wrapped up with my bandanna."

The next day went better. He would still moan, but it didn't seem as often or as loud. I did a heap of thinking while driving that team. How do I deal with Nation? Is he after the payroll? What is it with Molly, why is he using her? How will her father get along, now crippled for life? They were questions that I didn't have any answers for.

As we came out of the canyon into the valley I knew we were only a few miles from town. I glanced back at Johnson who was soundly sleeping. I sure hoped that the leg was better, it sure wouldn't do me any good if he were to die from blood poisoning while I was bringing him home. Hmpf, it wouldn't do him any good either, I thought with a dry chuckle.

By the town we were riding down main street there was some color back in his face. I took him straight to the doctor's office. Doctor Henry Jones was his name. He wasn't young, but he was new to the town and seemed to be a good man. His wife, Edith would help him in severe cases.

With some help, we were able to get Johnson into a bed in the backroom. I told the doc what had happened then gave him the almost empty bottle of laudanum. He mumbled something then turned to get his bag of tools.

Edith had come down to help, and I told them I was going to fetch his wife. "Wife!" exclaimed Doc. "Now who in the world is that?"

I began to explain as briefly as possible that he was working up in Silverton and that Helen Johnson, the owner of the eatery was his wife.

"My land," he said. "Well, go get her!"

His office was catty-cornered to the eatery so I left the wagon and hurried on over to get Helen. I thought it strange that Molly wasn't there, but I found Helen in the kitchen. There was only a couple of men at one of the tables. I told her what had happened and for her to go on down to the doc's to see him; that I would take care of the place.

After she left, I refilled the cups of the two men then stood there wondering about the Johnsons. About ten minutes later, Molly came bursting through the door into the kitchen. I could see anger all over her face. I stood right still, and she didn't see me.

"Molly," I whispered. Even the whisper made her jump.

"Miles," she moaned, "help us." She threw herself toward me and I grasped her, pulling her to me and holding her tightly.

"You hussy! Where did you go?" barked a voice from out front. I pulled Molly behind me then stood at the edge of the kitchen door. Standing in front of me was Ezra Nation, his hand touching scratches on his face.

"You!" he snarled.

"Get out, Nation!" I ordered.

He hissed, "Want to play this out now, Forrest? Think you can take me? Well, go ahead."

CHAPTER 37

Pushing Molly to the side, I then nodded with the side of my head for her to continue along the wall. The kitchen door was behind me, and Nation was standing in front of me.

He smiled, "Not yet, Forrest, but your time will come."

As he began to turn and walk away I hollered. "Nation, you can't stand it that I'm not afraid of you."

Spinning back around he snarled, "You afraid of dying, Forrest?"

I looked him in the eye, "None of us get out of this world alive, so, no, I'm not afraid of dying. I have a Redeemer whom I trust."

His face filled with rage. Faster than anything I had ever seen he drew and fired. I didn't flinch.

The rage went out of his face, and he paled. With eyes wide open in disbelief he stared at me. I drew my pistol, cocked the hammer pointing the gun at him. "Afraid of dying, Nation?"

I released the hammer and holstered my pistol.

He swallowed and muttered, "Your time will come, one day, Forrest."

I stopped his talking. "Get out, Nation. Go your cowardly way and heed your own words," I spit out the words then added. "Don't come back in this establishment, your presence taints the food."

He spun and left. I turned, taking a step toward Molly who was standing against the wall. "Stop, don't move," she said in almost a whisper. She looked at me, then where the bullet hit the door to the kitchen. "How? It's impossible."

I never thought about Nation missing. But something must have happened and when I looked at where the bullet was in the door I trembled. She looked at my coat and there wasn't a bullet hole, only the groove of a bullet that went under my armpit. It was the only place where he could have missed.

Taking her by the hand, I led her to the table. I needed a cup of coffee. "Just a case of a miracle. Long time ago I realized that I needed to put my life in the Lord's hands and let Him take care of me. Sometimes I haven't done such a good job, but He has always been there. I'm not leavin' this earth until He says for me to join Him up yonder."

"There surely have been times," I continued after pouring the two of us a cup of coffee, "I questioned the way He was doin' His job, but by and by, I realized that He knew what was best and I could trust Him."

"You should be dead, Miles," uttered Molly. "Ezra shot to kill you."

I smiled and had to laugh just a little. "Yeah, he was some surprised that it didn't quite work out thataway."

Her hand was trembling as she picked up her cup to sip, and it began to shake even more. I was afraid she'd spill her coffee so I reached out to steady her. After placing the cup back on the table, her hand flew to her mouth and she began to sob. "Ohhh, Miles, what have I done? What has my family done? And now, you're in danger because of us, because of me."

I forgot that I still had my hat on my head, so I took it off laying it on the chair next to me. "Molly, I've seen plenty of danger. I've had my share of spills and hard knocks, and it seems that when the Lord allows a person the opportunity to help others he should take it."

I reached to take a swallow of coffee. After a couple of deep swallows I placed the cup back on the table. "Molly, I feel in here," bringing my hand to my chest, "that this is my calling. This is what I'm supposed to do with my life."

She didn't say anything, but got up to refill my cup. When she was pouring my coffee, I thought, "I could get used to this." I looked over to the counter in toward the register and pointed. "Is that a razzberry pie, I see?"

Smiling she went to get me a piece. "Mother found some she had canned so decided to make a pie." She brought me a piece and I cut into it, the red berry juice running out on my plate.

I ate several bites, when Molly remarked, "I've never seen a person smile as he eats."

My smile increased as I looked at her, but I remembered my manners and kept my mouth shut. I was down to my last bite when there was a ruckus at the back door. I looked at Molly and she shrugged her shoulders. "What now?" I thought as I pulled out my pistol.

There was some crashing and Molly was ready to jump up to go see, but I grasped her arm to hold her at the table. The kitchen door was kicked open and Dan Johnson was thrust out landing on the floor with a heavy groan. Nation was holding tightly to Helen, glaring at me.

He walked to Molly's father. "Johnson!
Changing your name doesn't change who you are."
He looked at Molly with that evil smile. "This is my old
saddle pard. How's the knee, Buckley?" Then he
gave it a kick.

Johnson groaned. Looking at him I thought he
might pass out.

"Oh, and I know Helen, too. She was sweet on
me once, before Dan appeared on the scene." He
stepped back to grab her. "She was sweet on lots of
folks if I recall, until Dan took her away. Dan and I
were Quantrill's lieutenants; he gave the orders and
we made sure that the gang carried them out. Now,
Molly, come to me!"

She hesitated and Nation drew his gun placing
the barrel against Helen's head. "Now, Molly!" he
ordered.

"Stay!" I barked. I still had my heavy coat on;
when I heard the commotion I picked up the Greener
and hid it under my coat.

Nation grinned, oh, I recognized that evil grin,
then he pushed the barrel into the side of Helen's
head bringing a gasp from her and cocked the
hammer.

"Molly," he said in an evil whisper.

"Don't move," I said to her. "Trust me."

I moved slowly toward Nation. "Forrest, I'm
tired of you. Maybe it is time for you to depart."

He moved the gun from Helen's head pointing it
my direction as I stepped toward him. He hadn't seen
the shotgun under my coat. I was about ten feet from
him and lifted it with both barrels cocked. It sort of
caught him by surprise.

"You tried once," I said then added, "'Fraid to die, Nation? You move that gun an inch and if I see that finger even begin to tighten, they'll have to pick your pieces off the floor. Best thing for you to do right now is uncock that gun and holster it."

I was concerned about Helen being so close. I watched as she slowly inched away and a bead of sweat appeared on Nation's lip. I could tell he wanted to shoot, but there is something about the eyes of a double-barrel shotgun staring you in the face only a few paces away. "Buckley or Johnson—it don't make a difference. But your kind can never understand— the heart can be changed. There is a God who hears the cry of the heart."

He eyes glazed; I thought for a moment that he was going to try it. To my relief he holstered his gun. Looking at me he spat, "You're weak, Forrest. Next time, next time you won't know when it's coming."

"Nation, get out," I said stepping closer. "You're plumb scarin' me to death."

He rushed out in a fury and I breathed a huge sigh of relief. "Molly, check on your mother." I went then to Dan helping him to a chair. I could tell he was in pain.

"I thought I was rid of that life," he breathed.

"Listen, Dan, the past is always there, but you don't have to stare it in the face."

"We'll have to pack up and leave; go far away, so far he won't be able to find us."

"Why?"

He lifted his head to look at me. "I can't fight him, especially like this." He seemed resigned to his fate.

"I can," I answered softly then looked at Molly. This was a part of my life that she hadn't really seen much, but there is a time to fight and defend, and this was it. She had to take me—all of me. There are times when guns and violence that come with them are necessary to bring justice.

"Why?" he asked softly.

I looked at Molly once more. "Because I'm called to help; because you're a friend."

CHAPTER 38

"Molly, stop! Where are you goin'?"

She was headed for the door. "I have to get the doctor for Dad," she answered.

"Come over here," I ordered. "Nation may still be outside. I'll go get Doc Jones, you sit here by your Dad with the shotgun. If Nation comes through that door just cock the hammer and pull the trigger; there ain't no need to aim, just point it at him."

There was no sign of Nation, of which I was glad, and I retrieved the doctor. He patched up Dan's leg with a new bandage. No more damage had been done, just more pain. After he left, Johnson told me some of his story of riding with Quantrill, Nation at his side.

"Ezra and I were pretty good friends. We rode together, caroused together, killed together and loved the same woman. One day he took me down to his place near Poplar Bluff and I met his girl." He pointed over at Helen. "I was immediately smitten by her. I snuck off a few times after that to see her, causing her affections to drift from Ezra."

"Several things happened at once: Quantrill was killed. Helen found religion, and Nation found out about us. Fortunately for me, he went on a rage and a killing spree, then got drunk and passed out for a couple of days. Long enough for me to elope with Helen and leave the country. We headed for the gold fields at Cherry Creek and then up to Idaho Springs. Ezra didn't follow; he stayed the course of the war and from what I heard escaped at war's end to Indian Territory."

I was puzzled. Where did Molly fit into this. She had said that she was ten and had a crush on Nation. I was ready to ask when Johnson continued.

"We were in Colorado a few months when Helen drug me to a tent-meeting where I found religion that night. Reading the Bible I saw where we were given a new name, so I took it for real and we became Johnson. I hoped never to hear the name Buckley again. I figured Mad Dan Buckley died that night at the altar in that tent-meeting."

I had heard such stories. It seemed in the West there were the extremes with few in-between. There was that lawless group like Nation, and there were those who served the Lord. Many times they might ride side-by-side. The West and the Lord had a way of giving folk a fresh start. Of course, it is up to the person to take advantage of the opportunity.

"Molly?" I asked.

"She is mine," he declared. "Not biologically, but I raised her since Helen and I were married. You'll have to ask Helen about her birth-father, but Molly is mine," he said, then shook his head. "Don't you now see? I have to leave, for their sakes."

"You're in no shape to travel, and you can't outrun Nation." I looked him straight in the eye. "Time to face your past and stop runnin' from it. Trust in the Lord and leave Nation to me. Now, that's not to say to let your guard down; you keep a gun handy and Molly close by."

Rubbing my chin I had some hunches and one was that Nation had other things on his mind besides Molly. I didn't rightly know why he shot Dan, that part didn't make any sense.

"Helen, why don't you make some fresh coffee. I need to run an errand and then will be back for some," I said then walked to the door. I had to see Jim Hill.

"You what?" he exclaimed when I told him that I wanted Dan Johnson to ride with me as guard. "Is he fit to ride that far? You said he had a busted knee."

I nodded, "If he can sit in a chair he can sit inside the coach. An extra gun would help if we are attacked," I argued, the asked. "Who's the driver?"

"It was supposed to be Bells, but he came down with the gout. I pulled Rancid Simpson from the Cortez route. Bill Wilson is the messenger."

He began to scratch his head with his forehead turning into furrows. "I'm not allowing any passengers," he paused, "it's a big payroll, upward over fifty thousand dollars."

Jim informed me that the stage would leave at 9:00 the next morning. Now I had to convince Dan to come with me. With some buffalo robes we could make it fairly comfortable. I hadn't informed Jim of Dan's previous relationship with Nation.

On the way back to the eatery I stopped at the telegraph office. Stan Offut looked up when I entered, "Oh, hello Miles," he greeted me. "I was just going to send Tommy to find you. Here's a telegram." He reached over the counter to hand me the note. It was from Cook.

Nation is poison—STOP--Wanted in California—STOP--bring him to me for extradition—STOP—beware and be careful." --Cook

Now I had some legal backing to take Nation. That is, if I could take him.

We had Dan all snug and comfortable in the coach. It didn't take much to persuade him to come. Both Helen and Molly were deadset against it, but it was something he felt he had to do. I didn't like leaving the two women alone, but I figured that Nation would be somewhere along the road waiting for the stage.

Molly was very solemn as I climbed aboard the stage. Dan and I both had shotguns and rifles with us. I smiled at her and winked as Rancid let out a boisterous yell, "Harrupptyaw!" The stage jerked then started down the road.

There was a couple of stations along the way, but we would stay only at one to get four hours sleep. If they didn't hit us at the station or before, then I reckoned it would be off Molas Pass.

Rancid was a good driver, I had ridden with him before. He knows how to work a team, but the road would be rough since this was the first stage to travel since the passes were open.

It made me recall a trip I took with Rancid coming from Cortez. I was riding messenger and we were moving along until the stage hit a hole in the road. The front wheel just snapped and the coach hit hard. I remember grabbing for the seat and barely hanging on. Johnson must have seen my actions.

"What are you thinking about?" he questioned.

It was then I realized that in my daydreaming I had grabbed hold of the edge of the seat. I commenced to tell him my story as we moved closer to Molas Pass:

"The wheel was broken and one of the animals was down, but at least the stage didn't roll over."

"Shore didn't see that hole," Rancid muttered, along with a few other things. I jabbed him and reminded him of the passengers. We were carrying a light load, two ladies and one man.

"I'll check on the passengers while you check the horse," I said, then walked to the coach door.

He nodded and ambled toward the downed animal. I opened the door to the stage hoping that it didn't topple as one was getting out. The passengers were all right, just a little shaken and on edge.

I helped the older lady from the stage and she was blubbering some nonsense about making it to Durango by tomorrow to catch the train. As I was helping the younger lady a gunshot went off, and she near leaped into my arms. She sighed and was flustered a bit.

"Let her down, you oaf!" cried the old lady. "Quit man-handling her! I"ll see you are fired."

I was sore tempted to drop her, but then it wasn't her fault she ended up in my arms, so I gently eased her down then tipped my hat. I figured the man could tend to himself so I went to Rancid.

Seeing the horse I knew what the shot was for. The horse had broke its leg somehow, so Rancid put it out of its misery. He was rubbing his jaws. "Way I figure it, we're about two hours from Mancos. They'll wait at least an hour not knowing if we're just late. Guess we ought to make a fire and get a little comfortable; it's gonna get a mite chilly," he said to no one in particular, then looking at me, "Think you can hunt us up some vittles?"

Rancid moved away, "I'll get the fire started and put coffee on, you see what you can find."

Forty minutes later I returned to a nice fire with a couple of rabbits. Not much to eat among five, but it would take the edge off our hunger.

Then the old woman piped up, "I'll not eat a bite of one of those rodents!"

"Don't worry, Ma'am," said Rancid. "I'll take care of yuh." He had a large frying pan and in it were a couple of steaks. "Let me get these started, and I'll find my little poke of salt."

I looked at his fare, then said, "I think I'll broil up these rabbits then you can take your pick."

The elder lady spike up, "You think I'll eat that when this kind gentleman has juicy steaks sizzling? You are not only an oaf, but an ignoramus as well."

Rancid smiled when he heard her call him a gentleman. He, the man, and the old woman partook of the steaks and despite her apparent well up- bringing I could hear her smacking her lips. The younger lady looked at me, and I shook my head.

"I think I'll try a little, of, oh, I don't know your name."

"Forrest, Miss, Miles Forrest."

"I'll have a bite of Mr. Forrest's rabbits.

"This is magnificent!" exclaimed the old woman. "I didn't know you could carry steak on the stage."

"They're a gift from Bernice," he said smiling.
"Bernice? Is that your wife?"
"Oh, no, Ma'am," Rancid replied soberly.
"Bernice is the horse I had to shoot."
Well, let me tell you the old woman lost it right there. With her puking, coughing, and sputtering, well she wasn't very lady-like."

I thought that Dan was going to have a laughing jag over my story. We were half-way up the pass when I beckoned for Rancid to stop.

CHAPTER 39

Then reality hit us. A few minutes before we were laughing and carrying on telling stories, but now, within the hour we could all be dead. Our carefree attitudes had become solemn.

After Rancid stopped the stage, I got out then hollered up to Bill. "You and Rancid are prime targets. Are you ready for this?" I hated for them to be so out in the open.

He nodded at me. "I'll take care of it."

I knew he would do his best. "You're call depending upon what they do," I replied then looked over at Rancid. He appeared to be placid with a firm look to his face. Only God knew what was going to happen.

"How many do you reckon there are?" asked Bill rubbing at his chin.

"I don't know for sure, I would surmise that there would be four or five, maybe more.

When I stepped back inside the coach Dan was checking the rifles, making sure they were loaded and ready for action.

Rancid snapped the reins when he saw the door close and the coach started off with a jerk. After we began to descend from the Pass, the land opened up. No longer were there walled canyons so they would come at us from the timber. Hitting the stage here would give several options for escape.

Topping the summit and moving down I could see where the land began to open up with the towering peaks that surrounded Silverton in the background.

Rancid had the horses trotting at a nice pace when out of the trees, from both sides came six horsemen firing wildly. They were too far for our shotguns to do any damage so we held our fire trying to be patient.

I recognized Nation right off in his black attire. "Hmpf," I muttered, "Wiggins and Trundel. Nation sure picked himself a quality outfit."

Then came the blast of a shotgun. It surprised me, but Dan was anxious. It stopped them for a minute, but that was all. Nation saw that it was Dan and even from our distance I saw an evil smile appear on his face.

I laid the Greener in front of me to pick up a rifle. Aiming it I fired, knocking Trundel off his horse. Rancid hadn't stopped but then the riders came hard, I heard Wilson cut loose, then a yelp from him as he fell from the stage. Rancid stopped the team, and we began our fight in earnest. He slide down to get underneath the stage.

Another of the outlaws went down. I saw something that I had never seen before. There was some foolish rider going round and round in circles with his horse, firing in whichever direction.

Our aim must have been true for we were taking our time, looking for targets and someone, either myself or Rancid knocked another out of the saddle.

"Let's get out of here!" hollered the rider near the fool riding in circles. I looked at Nation, he hesitated then took off up toward the Pass.

I jumped from the stage to check on those we had put down making sure of them. One man I had never seen before, but Wiggins was dead and when I came to Trundel, he stared up at me trying to speak, but passed on into perdition.

"Forrest," hollered Rancid. "Over here."

He was standing hovering over the body of Bill Wilson. He had been shot once in the side and took another bullet in the side of his neck. I looked at Rancid shaking my head.

"Didn't know him well," he said. "He didn't seem like a bad guy, too bad, I'd liked to have ridden with him again." He then reached down to pick up an arm and I joined him to drag him to the stage.

I opened the door. "Sure hate to do this to you Dan, but I need to put Bill's body in here," I said, then added. "Won't be long, only a couple of hours."

After depositing Bill, Rancid poked me on the shoulder. "What about them?"

I didn't like the idea of leaving them to the varmints so I looked around for their horses. I spotted two and moved slowly toward them hoping I wouldn't scare them for I was sure they were skittish from the shooting.

Rancid helped me tie Trundel and Wiggins on one as they were scrawny. The other man, the one none of had seen before was tied on the others then we tethered them to the back of the stage.

No more problems arose on the journey. We unloaded the payroll at Wells Fargo and our work was finished—at least for this trip. We left the next morning to head home, this time with passengers, two men and a lady. I rode with Rancid as messenger.

I knew that Dan was hurting, but he managed to hide it well. From time to time he would take a nip from the laudanum. I was thinking that he was becoming too dependent upon it.

Two days later we pulled in front of the hotel in Durango to let the passengers off, then went to the eatery to unload Dan. I told Molly that I was going to ride with Rancid to the livery to help him unhitch.

As we rode up, Gibby came out to meet us. "I'll help Rancid," then he pointed inside the livery. "There's a man waitin' to see yuh in there."

Unbuttoning my coat, I made sure I could get to my pistol loosening the thong off the hammer. I carried the Greener in my left hand and slowly entered the barn. There was a man leaning back in a chair next to the stove sipping coffee. His eyes caught mine and a grin creased his face.

I watched his hand move. "Been waitin' for yuh" He reached in his pocket, took something out flipping it toward me. I let it hit the ground.

"Pick it up, Miles. You'll need it," he said.

Now I grinned after hearing the voice. "Thought you were cowboyin' up in Wyomin', I said as I reached down to pick up the object. It was a badge.

"Too cold," he simply stated. "Rode back to Denver and went to work for Cook. I was somewhat upset that I never caught up to those robbers I was chasing from Idaho Springs and didn't want to be marshalin' no more."

He stood up from the chair. "Yuh know how Cook can talk yuh into something? After a nice porterhouse he pulled me down to the governor's office and convinced Governor Pitkin to give me a badge." He opened his coat, "Genuine tin—says U.S. Marshal and yur my duly appointed deputy. Pin it on and we'll go get Nation. There's more than a few federal warrants for him."

I started to say that I didn't want the badge, but Elias was up and out the door heading for the eatery. "Comin'?" he asked.

We had just walked out from the livery when we heard the shots. It caused us to run toward the sound. When we got to the eatery the door was locked. Looking through the windows it seemed like everything was alright. I headed down the street then to the back of the eatery where their little house was with Elias following. That was a different story. The door had been kicked open.

Slowly I moved through and to the left, Elias went right. It was silent. Elias lit the lamp on the table and my attention went to the rocker by the fire. Dan Johnson sat there—dead. I went to the bedrooms, neither Molly or Helen were there.

"Nation!" I hollered.

Elias went outside. "Miles, tracks. There are five horses. Come looksee."

We both studied the tracks getting them etched in our minds. "Miles, go by the stage office, tell them you'll be goin' on a trip and I'll meet you at the livery. I'll have Toit saddled by the time you get there."

"Don't have Toit anymore; he died. Mine is an appaloosa; named him Hawk."

By the time I was there he had the horses saddled. We mounted, looked at each other when Elias asked, "Any idea of which way to travel? I know they didn't go west."

I pulled on my moustache. "Reckon they went back toward Silverton. Could have gone south into New Mexico, but I'm ponderin' a thought or two and I say we head north to the diggin's."

I prayed that I was right. I didn't relish the idea of Molly staying the night with Nation or any of his men. They were not far ahead of us, so we would have to travel warily.

Elias breathed, "We'll find them," then he paused with a sigh. "Another trail, partner. Seems like the good Lord puts us together for a purpose." He gave his old horse a nudge and Hawk followed.

CHAPTER 40

There were several tracks in the road, but it wasn't hard to find a group of five traveling together. We moved cautiously, but at a slow trot. I wasn't too afraid of them stopping to set up an ambush with the two women with them. However, the further we moved up into the canyon that could change.

After passing through Hermosa the grade became a little steeper, we were entering the canyon. Not far ahead the road would leave the river moving to the west. Gold and silver had been found throughout these mountains so there were mines and shacks scattered throughout. We had to move slower and watch that the group did not turn off.

Not long after Hermosa, maybe an hour there was a road moving off to the left. Not a road really, just two wagon tracks moving up a steep grade. I could see the road split between a slag pile and a pile of gravel. Someone was or had been working a claim.

We stopped before cresting the little ridge formed by the slag pile. "They could be waitin' for us, yuh know," stated Elias stoically.

I looked over at him and smiled. "Why don't we go see." I gave Hawk a slight nudge to move along the ruts, stopping him when I could see over the ridge.

There was an area that flattened out for about thirty yards. To my far right was a small, covered stall to which a little corral was attached. There were six horses in the corral. A few feet from the corral was the shack. It was rather small and I wondered how six people would even fit in there. Across some open ground, back in the hillside was the opening to a mine.

Elias was shaking his head. "I don't like it. That shack is so small that if'n we go in there blazin' the women stand a good chance of bein' hit."

I dismounted, then took Hawk back down the road a bit to drape the reins over a limb of a pine. Elias followed suit, then we walked to the right so that we would come up next to the stall.

It was a steeper climb with the gravel causing us problems, and we had to succumb to going up on our hands and knees. Each of us holding a shotgun didn't make it any easier, but eventually we made it. We stopped next to the back wall of the stall to catch our breath. The exertion in the high altitude had made the climb more difficult.

"Stay here," I ordered.

"That's not goin' to happen," came the tart reply from Elias.

I put my hand up to my mouth to quiet him. "I've a feelin' about this. You stay back; you're my secret weapon. I'm sure there's someone in the stalls."

He sighed then nodded in agreement, and I moved from my position acting as if I were sneaking into the stalls. I knew that there was someone there, I could feel it in my gut, plus I thought I heard someone humming or singing.

Passing the first stall, I could see that it needed cleaning. Then as I went past the next one, there was the sound of a giggle. "Impson was right. He figured you'd be along."

I stopped, now it was crucial. I sure hope they didn't tell the guard to shoot on sight. "I'd plug you," he giggled again, "but I want to see yur face when you see that girl of yourn. Besides Ezra wants your company. Give me yur gun and let's go."

Turning my gaze to a man I recognized from the attempted holdup. He was the one acting all crazy, and from his movements I figured he was a load short in the head. "I may look as dumb as an ol' fence post, but no way am I goin' into Nation's lair without my gun."

The muscles in his cheek twitched, the poor boy was trying to think it through. He began waving his gun around and I was afraid he might shoot. "Ezra wouldn't like it if you didn't take me to him."

His eyes sort of rolled around in his head, then he shook it hard. Finally he nodded, "All right, but you leave the shotgun."

I leaned it against the outside wall of the stall then started toward the shack with the man following a distance behind. Approaching the shack, it was then I noticed a small covered lean-to that was partially filled with wood. There was Molly tied to a post, but I didn't see signs of Helen. Coming closer I saw the foot of someone who was laying on the ground. It must be Helen.

"Hey, Ezra! I got him!" hollered the man.

The door opened, Nation walked out followed by a stockier man who I assumed was Impson McCracken. "Welcome, Forrest. Well, it looks as if your day has finally come." He looked to my guard congratulating him, "Good job, Brit. I'm proud of you."

I glanced at the man and he was beaming from the praise. But then he harshly said, "But I see you let Forrest keep his gun."

Brit's lip quivered, "But, but I made him leave the shotgun in the stall."

Nation didn't pay any more attention to him, but turned to me. "How do you like my little attraction all trussed up for market? She'll bring a fine price up at the dens in Silverton, don't you think?" he laughed seeing the anger rise to show in my face.

"Where's Helen?"

"Well, she was a little impertinent so Joe had to slap some sense into her. She's not hurt bad, just unconscious."

"Joe?" I thought, the rider of the fourth horse. I couldn't worry about him now.

Nation had his thumbs hooked in his gunbelt while Impson moved toward where Molly was tied up. I looked at her, she seemed to be all right. She was gagged; I could only see her eyes staring at the scene unfolding in front of her.

Nation began to explain. "Since my old friend Dan Buckley stole Helen from me I thought I'd make some money off his girl and sell her. I just wish he was alive to see the show, but perhaps he's watching from the devil's lair."

My hand was poised, ready to grab my gun when my companion whacked my elbow with the barrel of his rifle bringing laughter from Nation.

"Don't hurt him, Brit. I want to see him fall when my bullet pierces his heart."

My left hand reached over to touch my elbow where Brit hit me. I moved my arm a little keeping it lose. I wasn't going to go down without a fight.

There was a moan from the shed. It was Helen. "Go help her up, Brit. I want her to see all that is going to happen, since Dan isn't here."

Helen began to sob. "Ezra don't. If you ever had feelings for me, don't."

"Shut up!" he snarled. "If you don't quit that whimpering I'm going to give you to Joe and then Brit can have you."

Nation turned to me. "Forrest, it's time."

He let forth a bellow of laughter when a blast from a shotgun startled him. I didn't hesitate and drew my gun. Even with the distraction I wasn't fast enough, my shot was just behind Nation's. I felt the bullet tear into me as I fired again, then a third shot. There was more gunfire off to my right, and I could feel a body fall to the ground, but my attention remained on Nation. He was lying on the ground in front of me, his blood mingling with the dirt forming a murky, ugly mud.

I walked up to him. "Afraid to die, Nation?" He gazed up at me, the smile was gone, and in its place was the look of terror.

He screamed, eyes widening, "Get him away!" then slumped, face going into the dirt as he took his last breath.

Turning toward Molly, I saw that Impson had a knife at her throat. I could see just a trickle of crimson coming from where the point of the knife touched her neck.

"Molly, my life is based on trust. Relationships must be based on trust. Do you trust me?" I didn't give her a chance to answer. I fired, my bullet striking the man in the forehead. He dropped the knife and fell to the ground.

I knew he had been shot, but I started walking toward Molly. She took a deep breath as I took out my knife and cut her down. She fell into my arms. As she held onto me, my attention was drawn to a man over in a dark corner to my right.

Hearing his steps I pointed the pistol in my left hand in his direction. "Easy there now, Pardner," came the voice. It was Elias.

CHAPTER 41

I was holding onto Molly, gun in one hand, knife in the other when I noticed Helen just standing there looking so very much alone. My eyes caught hers and I opened my left arm. She ran to me and all three of us hugged each other, Molly and her mother both crying.

"Miles," breathed Helen, "take us down to Hermosa. I can't bear the thought of spending the night here."

"It'll be dark when we get there," I responded, releasing her.

She was still sobbing and heaving when she answered, "I don't care. I can't stay here."

Elias had been busy checking the dead. He came to stand beside me placing his hand on my shoulder. "Pard, this is a bloody and dirty business," he said with disgust in his voice. "Go ahead with the women, I'll take the bodies on down to Durango and will meet up with you some time tomorrow."

It wasn't until then that Molly realized that I was shot and bleeding. She moved away from me then saw that her dress had blood on it as well as her arm.

"Miles!" she exclaimed as she pulled my shirt out of my pants to examine my side.

I looked at her as she checked the wound. "Another shirt with holes in it," I quipped.

"This is not a joke!" she said angrily. "You could have been killed."

I looked over at Elias who just smiled and shrugged his shoulders. "I'm going to saddle their horses. Oh, by the way, there was another jasper that had a bead on you. I had to blast him with the shotgun."

"His name was Joe," I replied.

"Joe what?"

It was my turn to shrug. "I don't know, Joe something, but at least the gang that robbed the Idaho Springs stage has been brought to justice. I wonder where the money is?"

Elias came me a puzzled look. "They couldn't have spent it all in a year, could they?"

"Be still!" ordered Molly. "I'm trying to clean this wound. The bullet never entered just cut a groove in your side, but it's still bleeding."

"Bandage it up, I'll get it looked at in Hermosa. You and Helen go get your things."

"This is all we have, Miles," said Helen. "I'll take their coats, they won't be needing them."

"No!" she exclaimed emphatically. "I won't, I can't wear them."

I thought for a moment. "Check inside for blankets. It'll be cold, and you'll need something."

Elias was busy packing the men over their saddles for the trip. As he was leading the horses back to the shack he tossed me the Greener. "Here, you might want this."

He moved on down the road with his gruesome pack. Helen had found a couple of blankets and had made ponchos out of them. A few minutes later we were on the road.

We stayed the night in Hermosa where Molly cleaned and bandaged my wound. Another scar to add to my collection. Helen was very quiet, but I couldn't blame her none. She had seen her husband killed, a man from the past was ready to throw her and Molly to the dogs. Yes, she had been through quite an ordeal.

The next morning on our way to Durango, she rode up next to me. "I would like to take Dan's body back to Missouri to bury him."

"I guess that's possible. Better check with the undertaker though," I replied. She then dropped back to ride next to Molly.

As we rode into town, Elias was there to meet us. "The house has been cleaned up," he told me. "I sent a telegram to Cook notifying him of McCracken."

He walked with us as I led them to the house. Molly dismounted, but Helen stayed on her horse wanting to go directly to the undertaker. For some reason Molly had become very quiet and distant. I asked Elias to stay with her while I took Helen to see the undertaker.

Paul Parker, the undertaker, was a middle-aged man. Thin, almost gangly, but not tall. He was very cordial and courteous, and said that he could pack the body in salt, then asked when she wanted to leave. Helen told him the sooner the better. Nodding his head letting her know he understood, he said that he would take care of the tickets.

"Two," Helen replied. "Winona."

"Three," I said interrupting. "I'm goin' with you."

She didn't protest, but did ask to be left alone as she wanted to pay her respects to Dan. I left to join Elias and Molly. I was at the front door and when I entered I saw Elias pointing his finger at Molly.

"Girl, yuh better wake up to the ways out here. Killin' is hard, and it wears on a man inside all of his life even if it is justified. Miles has seen rightly more than his share. He doesn't need you backin' away from him. If you could see the scars he carries in his soul, well, maybe you would be more kind-hearted toward him. A woman shouldn't try and go changin' a man; her job is to take him as he is, support him, and help make him better."

I interrupted with a cough. "Helen is staying a bit longer. She has tickets for Winona, she wants to bury your father back home."

"I better go pack then," she said walking away not acknowledging me.

Elias was scratching his head then motioned for us to go outside. "What's with her?"

"I think there was just too much killin' at one time for her," he replied. "Miles, I need to ask yuh something. Do yuh love her?"

It sort of surprised me hearing that come from his mouth. I twisted my moustache then rubbed my chin. "I have those feelin's."

"No, Miles, it has to be more than feelin's! It has to be real, from the heart, not just an emotion," he was becoming excited.

"You turnin' preacher?" I questioned. He stopped his talking, then smiled.

"Elias, I'm not quick to use my gun. In fact, I'd rather not use it to settle my quarrels. Maybe I have used it too much, but never without just cause. Maybe one day there won't be a need for a person to have a gun for protection; maybe one day man will get a bit smarter."

He looked at me then off to the distance before answering. "Don't think so, Miles. If I read the Good Book right, the days are goin' to be more evil than we've seen. Things may change some, but I wouldn't be fool enough to put my guns away."

Pausing he turned his attention back to me. "Yur goin' with them, aren't you?"

"That's my plan," I replied, then reached inside my coat for the badge. "Here, take this. I'll talk with you later. I need to see Jim Hill about takin' time off. He might fire me."

He smiled. "Then keep the badge. It wasn't a loaner. When you get back contact Jens Blasco in Denver if I'm not available. He is the U.S. Marshal for the region."

"Will I see you before I leave?" I asked. We had parted several times in the past so I knew it was coming.

"Leavin' on the last train out tonight," he informed me, then reached out his hand. I nodded slightly then took it. "Give her time, Miles, give her time."

He started to walk away, then after five steps he turned. "If I don't see yuh again down here, I'll see yuh up yonder," he said pointing to the sky.

EPILOGUE

After the first hour on the train the barrier that had been up between Molly and me was broken down. We had to change trains in Kansas City and again in Springfield, but the trip went fine.

We talked most of the way, except when we weren't sleeping, and Helen joined in with our conversation. She didn't seem remorseful and I think the talking was therapy to her. She told about Ezra and Dan and their friendship during the war, then how Dan stole her away. Much of what she spoke of Molly didn't know.

Molly did question my toting around the Greener. "Why must you carry that thing everywhere?" she asked one time when I moved it from the seat. In fact, the conductor even questioned that I shouldn't be carrying it on the train until I showed him my marshal's badge.

"Habit," was my simple reply. She gave a little grunt, then turned to look out the window for a little while. It was about the only time one of us wasn't talking on the trip.

Upon arrival in Winona, Helen's sister Alice was there to meet us. It was the first time they had seen each other in over ten years. We waited until the local mortician came to get the body, telling us that the funeral would be tomorrow morning.

Alice looked much like Helen, but didn't have the wrinkles around her eyes that come from worrying. Also her hands were not as rough as her sister's. Her husband, Clem made a good living working at the bank in town. He couldn't get off work to meet us but would be home for supper.

Alice and Helen were chatting up a storm as we walked to Alice's home. Molly and I followed. I reached out and took her hand. She didn't object, but looked up at me and smiled.

Their house wasn't fancy, but it sure was better than an old shack up in the mountains. But I learned a long time ago, that a house and land doesn't make a home. It takes work, effort, sweat, tears and prayer to make a home.

I found that Clem was a gracious man. He enjoyed conversing, though his experience was limited. He was too young to be in the War, and his life consisted of living in Winona though he was born outside St. Louis. He was about my height, a little heavier perhaps because of a softer lifestyle.

Clem had a carriage that would only fit three people so after breakfast I went to the livery to see if there was something I could rent for the funeral. Fortune was with me, for the owner had an old buggy and a horse that was trained. They cost me two dollars for the day, but I was glad Molly was sitting by me on the way to and from the gravesite.

If was a nice funeral, if a funeral can be nice. Dan had told me that he had made his peace with the Lord several years back so that feeling of judgment wasn't hanging over us. The preacher did a good job, but to tell the truth I don't remember much of what he said, as I had other things on my mind.

Helen didn't know anyone but Alice in town, so the attendance was small. A few friends of the Musgraves showed up out of respect to the family. Alice had met Dan, but it was back in his wild days.

Some folks from the church brought dinner over for us then politely left. It was not a time of remorse, but one of reunion. Mostly there were smiles and laughter. Helen and Molly had done most of their mourning on the trip.

That evening, we were sitting in the living room with a small fire burning in the fireplace. Alice was serving us coffee in these fancy cups that I struggled with putting my finger through the handle. The conversation was light, but then Helen spoke up.

"I've been thinking seriously about this, and have already talked with Alice and Clem—I'm planning on staying in Winona."

Molly threw her hand up to her mouth. It can as a surprise to her. "What about the eatery?"

Helen smiled, "I'm giving that to you. Run it, sell it—it's yours."

I pulled the cup off my finger, then set it and the saucer on the edge of the mantle after I stood. "That sorta settles things in my mind, so I gotta act fast."

The four of them look at me puzzled. I went over and touched Molly on the shoulder. "Molly, you better get busy. With your mother staying here that means we need to get married next week before we leave."

"Married!" they all said simultaneously in different tones of voice.

"Miles," Molly whispered, then I lifted her by the hand from her chair, pulled her to me and kissed her.

"There, that settles it," I said smiling releasing her then looking at my audience. Clem was smiling, Alice was stifling a laugh with her eyes wide, and Helen was there touching her lips with both hands together as if in prayer.

"Oh, Miles!" Molly breathed then pulled me to her kissing me again. It was settled.

ABOUT THE AUTHOR

This is the eleventh novel by Donald C. Adkisson who started writing as a hobby. His purpose is always, first of all, to bring glory to Christ, but also to inspire and write for enjoyment.

As a historian with a M.A. in education/U.S. History from Northern Kentucky University, he would tell you that most of the stories and movies that depict the West only show part of it. True, there were the saloons, brothels, and other dives, but there was also the good side of town—the churches, the work places of the common people. Many of the people considered themselves to be Christians which he tries to make a focal point in his writing.

He was born and raised in Boulder, Colorado and met his wife, Annie Baker, while attending Evangel University in Springfield, Missouri. Following graduation and six years in the U.S. Air Force, he began his career in education where he spent thirty-nine years as a teacher, coach, and administrator.

Annie and Don have two children and four grandchildren. They have a little cottage in the woods of East Texas near Coldspring.

Since 2001, Don has written a daily devotion titled "Echoes From the Campfire" which may be found at www.irapaine.com with excerpts on Facebook. He has also published one devotional book, *Trails in the Wilderness.*

Call to Justice

D. C. Adkisson

Call to Justice

www.ingramcontent.com/pod-product-compliance
Lightning Source LLC
Chambersburg PA
CBHW061243120726
48001CB00001B/120